THE DECAPAPHI[illegible]

AND

OTHER STORIES

BY ALEX WEINLE

First published in Great Britain

By Charlotte Cottage Books Ltd 2012

ISBN: 1493703692
ISBN-13: 9781493703692

Alex Weinle writes speculative and literary fiction for which his work in science, commerce and computing in regions domestic and foreign have prepared him very poorly.

He lives in Cambridge in a cottage that consumes bulbs of unusual wattage.

Contents

The Decapaphiliac

(or Love in the Time of Cappuccinos)

Annie has red hair. She enjoys great success with friends and lovers due to her joviality, adequate looks and a developed air of the risqué. Despite these positives she has not yet found the ideal partner - but then this is real life where problems are always mixed in with the perfection - and ire is not so easy to remove from adore. The truth about life is complicated, indefensible and embarrassing. It is this facet of being that most people prefer served with a *jus de denial* and construct a veneer of delusion to help life along.

She had engineered several reasons to talk to Malcolm Spinx: a reason every time she handed him his morning coffee. Annie worked as a barista in the coffee shop across the road from Malcolm's office and each morning she made one espresso with just a little more love than the rest and she smiled a little wider than she did for anyone else.

As mentioned above: this is reality and though Annie had expected her ground work to pay off sooner or later, it did not. Malcolm was clearly attracted to her but something held him back. She saw his pupils expand that little bit when he spoke to her. He tried to be funny, sometimes succeeding, but could not or would not summon the courage to ask her out - even though she had made it clear that the answer would be yes. O yes.

After watching him across the rainy street to his office, she rested her head against the growling espresso machine, wiped the coffee oil from it and cleaned the milk from the sadly phallic steam pipe. Annie despaired for a few seconds. She knew full well that we live in a pickled world of imperfection and this was just a down lull in the proceedings, so she gathered herself together and took a moment to wash under her finger nails while assessing her situation: so far - so bad.

The next day after she delivered a meticulous good morning, she skipped the normal small talk with Malcolm pulled a pen from her top pocket and in front of him wrote her number and the phrase 'I love you and I'm hungry' on the cardboard band that kept customers' hands from being scalded. She popped the ring around the cup and handed him his coffee while smiling and wishing him a nice day. The stunned Malcolm wandered out of the shop onto the street then back into the shop and up to the counter.

"What time would you like to eat?"

"About seven-thirty? See you here?"

"Right."

So – Annie - not only a red head but a woman of resource as well. That evening she discovered Malcolm was no slouch himself. During dinner at an inexpensive, yet delicious and intimate restaurant, he demonstrated that he was funny, intelligent, humble and handsome by candlelight. Annie had considered herself in control of the situation but now she felt the inkling of free fall and the rush of dangerous attraction. She told him about parts of her life that she hoped would make her appear interesting and omitted the sections where she was a fool stuck in dead-end jobs or childish relationships.

He took her to her doorstep while a black cab rattled with diesel impatience and kissed her on the cheek. He thanked her for a wonderful night.

Was this gallantry, thought Annie, or had she somehow blown it with him by committing some unspeakable error? It seemed not, as Malcolm phoned her again and they enjoyed another meal. The calls and the dates continued: a concert, a play, meals and drinks. All the while that plummeting, chest-splitting feeling crept over Annie and pushed her up against Malcolm who looked at her as if she were every Hollywood star rolled into one. Still no sex though.

When Annie's frustration became too much to bear she decided that she would have to take the lead on this part of the relationship as well. Perhaps Malcolm had religious objections to sex. Perhaps he was insecure, perhaps. She couldn't wait any longer to find out. The next time they stepped out of a taxi she paid the driver and told him to take off. She man-handled her lover through the door, up the stairs and out of his shirt. They spent the night and a good portion of the next morning rolling around in bed together. In bed, on the floor and in the hallway. Annie became aware that Malcolm never reached a climax during all of their love-making.

"Is this a tantric trick? You not finishing off?"

"Its... no. I want to but I can't...it doesn't matter. I love being with you."

From that night on they were inseparable and rapacious. Annie moved into Malcolm's house after a week and they proved that the opposite of bored is not interesting: it is loved. Still Annie was bothered by her partner’s lack of orgasm despite his protests that it wasn't important. He was clearly capable of arousal - what was missing?

"It's not that you can't come right? I mean you have come before?"

"Yes, absolutely but it's when I'm thinking about something else."

"Something else? What is it? We can do that then. I'd do anything for you, you know that."

"No. You mean the world to me. I don't want to lose you over something as stupid as this. I don't want that happening." He inspected the paintwork on the window sill but Annie pushed herself under his nose and looked up into his eyes.

"Mal, I need you. No matter what you say: I can't leave you. Want to tie me up? Spank me? Dress me up like a cat? No problem; let's do it."

"It's not that easy, I don't know why I'm like this. I wish I could change. I've seen... people... about it but nothing helps. I'm doomed."

"How can I help if you won't tell me? Don't you see that really there isn't any choice about this? We both know it's a problem. We can let it fester in silence and sour every bit of our love or we can just face it together. I haven't ever been an ordinary kind of girl Mal, trust me enough to tell me."

"Yeah, I know you're right. It's just that once this cat is out of the bag I can't see anything ever being as – well as really *good* as it’s been over these last few weeks.” He stood up a little straighter as if bracing himself against a firing squad. “It's like this: I get turned on by women with no heads."

"I can be a bimbo for you Mal, hell I can borrow some of my sister's clothes to complete the effect."

"No Annie, really, no head at all; like Marie-Antoinette. Head missing. Decapitated."

She was shocked into sitting, trying to spin what she heard into some kind of sense.

"How do you get that? Have you ever..."

"No I've never done it. When I was a kid my dad worked at the print works – he used to bring home loads of dictionaries and misprints with pages missing or the covers on the skew. We had the complete Tin Tin books printed without the colour yellow. This once he brought back a great stack of glamour magazines that had been incorrectly guillotined: what can I say? I was a bag of seething hormones at the time. I sneaked some of the more titillating ones off to my room and did what teenage boys do best – to pictures of women with no heads. It's been the only thing that really does it for me since then. I guess you’ll want to leave now."

Annie considered for a moment the perfection/problem mix and rebounded with the resilience of bare-knuckle fighter.

"How about a bag?"

"I'm sorry - what?"

"You know like a black bag, I could put one over my head and it'll make me look sort of headless."

"Annie, I refuse to do that to you. It's demeaning. I won't."

The bag idea was very nearly an early success but towards the end Mal could hear Annie panting inside the bag and this seemed to shatter the illusion of headless-ness. This was followed by progressively more inventive and ultimately less successful attempts. In desperation Annie considered whether finally the perfection/problem mix might be too much for her to conquer. She knew how to act on the mythical subject of that valueless, non-existent and eternal commodity: love. She treated it with a gamekeeper's cunning and reasoned that nothing was compulsory in life, she could live without it or she could see what she was willing to put up with to have love. She consoled herself that there was some satisfaction to be had in refuting the conventional image of romance.

Her beloved's condition was stretching this concept to the limit, she wasn't pleasing herself with her decisions or the actions that she took part in. They were sacrificial: they were entirely for him. Was she just fostering a delusion that she was strong enough to carry this relationship?

It was then - in the eleventh hour of her despair - that a solution struck her.

When she saw Malcolm next at the coffee shop she handed him his drink and a business card.

Dr Leonard Talbot

Therapist

020 7946 0023

It was carefully squeezed between the cup and the cardboard ring holder. She stopped trying to solve the problem with cheap bedroom escapades and waited the suggested twelve weeks that her new advisor and partner in crime had proscribed.

It was a balmy evening when Mal came home and found Annie lounging about the flat in her underwear.

"I'm sorry my love – the sessions are over and in my heart I know that I still have the same problem. I can't pretend it wasn't nice to sit in the doctor's office and be honest about myself." He looked at the floor. "Lying there listening to him repeatedly telling me it isn't my fault. He just wanted me to sit still and relax. You know he talked more than any therapist I've ever known."

Mal dropped his briefcase and slumped into an armchair. He was at the end of his emotional reserves. He had bared his soul in every aspect to this medical professional that Annie had found, told every detail of his fantasy's development and confronted the aspect of loathing that he had for himself.

For an hour or more every day for twelve weeks he had been with the illustrious Dr Talbot. He poured out his life and suspicions and fears. The kind-faced therapist continually told him that he should relax and let whatever came to the surface just happen. The experience was so fatiguing that often he would fall asleep on the therapist's couch.

“Be not afeared my love.” Annie said and straddled his lap. “Things are not entirely as they may appear to be, you’ll have to forgive the doctor and I for a little deception.”

“Deception? Twelve weeks of failed counselling, what kind of deception could be worth that?” Mal asked.

“I suspect you may have slept through more of the sessions that you admit to my dear. You have been looking particularly well rested of late and such a powerful suggestion does take a very long time to reinforce. I can’t pretend that I haven’t been impatient to see the results myself.”

She produced another business card from her bra. It read:

Dr Leonard Talbot

Therapist, Hypnotist and Stage Performer

020 7946 0023

She chuckled. Annie clicked her fingers and said "I have no head."

She suspected but had not dared to hope the fulfilment of his oft repeated fantasy would ground it: reality can never live up to the dream and after nine or ten rampant doses of wish-fulfilment he held her in his arms and started talking.

"There's something you should know about the therapy Annie. I've been back to see Talbot and the doctor tells me it was so unusually effective because he combined the two things I most wanted in the world. He says my will for it to succeed completely ran rough shod over my waking mind's prudishness."

Annie nuzzled the pillow in a state of post-coital bliss.

"Rough shod. Very effective. Good therapy." She mumbled.

"Ok, well I suppose that might be obvious from an outside perspective but you know what really has sorted me out the most? He told me that the effect wouldn't last long without the booster sessions we were starting. He asked me straight out if I really wanted it to last any longer. He asked me that this morning."

Annie opened one unfocused eye in interest

“I'm telling you: I was flummoxed. Here we are doing the thing I’ve always dreamed of without nightmares of you running scared from me like I was Frankenstein’s monster and he asks me do I really want it to last any longer? Before I’d thought about it - I’d told him ‘No’ but every bit of me thought I wanted to say ‘Yes’. Talbot seemed genuinely overly pleased with himself. He told me to go home and enjoy it because someday I’d be his age.”

Annie sat upright – her fiery hair frizzed on one side from the pillow.

“What are you telling me?”

“I’m saying that last time you clicked your fingers nothing happened – most importantly that nothing *needed* to happen. I guess I’m going to have to get along with just the normal fantasies guys have from now on.”

Just at that moment Annie’s concept of the problem/perfection mix broke down. She sat bolt upright in bed in the hot summer bedroom and inspected his face for any trace of insincerity: there were no problems at all.

She crawled over him and got to within an inch of his all-so-pleased face.

“Which normal guys' fantasies?”

The Glasses Adjuster

In a back corner of the market place amongst the discarded fruit crates he sat on a teak box with a smart painted sign next to him that read 'Glasses Adjusted: One Pound'. He was dressed in a jacket and shirt, had a clean shaven face and tightly cropped hair. He waited. His face turned and smiled whenever he felt a potential customer was passing but otherwise was quite motionless.

The box on which sat on seemed to be from the orient, polished teak inlaid with reeds and lotus blossom. The side facing the market walk contained a hundred tiny drawers with a minute handles. Every handle was unique among its brothers and sisters: a bead of blue and gold glass, a pebble of tiger's eye, a glass bauble trapping a cumin seed and ninety-seven others.

The Glasses Adjuster was not a busy man. No one queued for his services and days passed without a person using his services. The Adjuster did not wear glasses.

From the maze of stalls appeared a tiny figure of a girl. She was bundled in a red duffle coat two sizes too big for her. Her wispy hair was ruffled by the wind amongst the stalls.

"Can you please fix these?" She asked.

"Let me look at them. Ah, this hinge has been warped. Take a seat while I set it straight? Isn't your mother about with you?" He said.

"She's buying veggies down there at the stall. I'll go straight back, right after you fix 'em, please… thank you."

Her voice announced this with a peculiar solemnity, the hood of the coat failed to hide a birthmark, a pinkish area from her chin, across her cheek to the corner of her right eye and up through the hairline at her temple.

"Aren't you polite? There's a special promotion for polite girls."

"Premotion? A premotion for girls?"

"Promotion, like ah, locomotion or… Well it's a little early for you to learn a word like that in school."

"I don't go to school now." She said. "Bullies. They don't like my face."

“That’s a shame. I’ve seen worse birth marks than yours. Where are those pliers – ah, here they are. Yes, I’ve definitely seen worse and more inflamed. And…”

“What is it?”

“My word isn’t that just amazing?”

“Is it my face? Sorry.”

“No - don’t be worried. You have the most remarkable Peczely Crowns.”

“P…Peczi who?”

“He invented Iridology. That’s when you try to determine the state of a person by looking at the pupil and iris in their eye.” The Adjuster meditated for a moment. “Here, you look at mine. What do you see? Not much eh? I was always cursed with the blandest of eyes but you? You’ve the rarest ones of all.”

The girl looked at the Adjuster's eyes.

“I do?”

The Adjuster lent back on his box-seat and tapped his chin with the watchmaker’s screwdriver, still holding the girls glasses in his other hand.

“I would say that there may be only one or two other people on the earth at this moment with Peczely Crowns, perhaps none at all. We had better take extra care if these glasses are going to frame the world's rarest and most beautiful eyes. I'm afraid you may deserve to see someone more qualified than me. The best opticians in the world wouldn't be good enough." Again he rummaged to somewhere deep in his memory waving the screwdriver like a miniature baton as he thought. "Can I suggest you try Japan? Doctor Myoshi is head and shoulders above the rest."

The girl was shocked.

"Japan? No I like you - not Myogi. I don't have to go do I?"

"Well, you could stick with me. It's a real honour. A little adjuster like me - in the back of a market - caring for the world's most beautiful eyes. I'll have to insist on refunding your money though – a commission like yours will undoubtedly bring in the business of the whole city."

He swept out his arm in a gesture that encompassed not just the market but the buildings beyond.

"For reals? And you really do think I'm pretty?"

"Unquestionably. You are the most beautiful girl in the world: no doubt the Almighty in his wisdom gave you that birth mark", he pointed carefully at the strawberry blemish, "so that men wouldn't fight with each other over you. Now that would be a terrible beauty wouldn't it?"

"I suppose so. Yea, he made me just right then?"

“He made you exactly right my princess. Now, try these on for me? Much better. Here’s your pound back with my thanks for your custom.”

The beaming look on her face wavered for a second with confusion as she looked at the coin in her hand.

“What about the premotion? Do I get it now?”

The Adjuster nodded and reached down to the minute drawers, opening one that had a tiny golden bell for a handle. He pulled it out and turned the contents into her hand. A tiny jade elephant stood proudly on the coin.

“His name is Bah Borom”, explained the Adjuster in a whisper, “and his job was to carry the royal family where ever they wanted to go in the whole world. He is brave, loyal and clever Take good care of him and he’ll take good care of you.”

The girl with the rarest eyes in the world put the figurine into the deep pocket of her duffle coat. She rushed off into the passages of the market to find her mother. For a fleeting moment a smile was on the lips of the Adjuster and then was gone as he returned to sitting and waiting.

All the long afternoon the Adjuster sat and meditated. Fragments of sunlight would break out and then be hidden again by the clouds. When the sun gazed down hard through a gap he turned his head slightly away and when the gloom returned she was walking toward him. She was tall but pale and thin. Without a word she brought out a spectacle case, one of the older ones that is a danger to your fingers when it closes. He prised open the lid and brought out the glasses, the lens of one orbit remained in the case.

“Do you use them only for reading?”

“No, I should wear them all the time but since the glass came out I’ve made do without them.”

“Were they dropped?” He asked.

“They were knocked off.” She said.

He examined the eyepiece and the frame, turning the items around on his lap. She stood over him and watched as he reshaped the arc of metal and tightened the midget screw of the hinge.

“This is the best I can do. You should get some new ones as soon as you can. A little jostle and the glass will probably come out again. Once you weaken the frame like that, it never really grips quite right with these lightweight sets.”

The Adjuster returned the glasses to their case and squeezed shut the lid. He went to hand them back to his customer and he saw a flicker of distress on her face, her mask had dropped for a moment. By the time she had pocketed the case her self-possession was back with her.

“Are they likely to be knocked off again?” He asked.

“No… I hope not, I don’t know. It isn’t important.”

“If it happens again you must bring them straight to me so that I can check the frames are ok. No charge, just to make sure they don’t become”, he looked intently at her, “impossible to repair.”

“That may not be so possible, next time.” She said and turned to leave.

“Hold on, let me give you something for those rings around your eyes. You aren’t getting much sleep? I don’t sleep well myself, just look at the bags under my eyes, caused by years of broken sleep cycles you know. Irreversible damage I suppose.”

The Adjuster peered at the drawers in the box and pulled out one with a cork bulb for a handle. Inside were two pills still in their wrapping.

“I use these when it’s really severe. Just a half should be enough for you. Two and even the heaviest man would be out for a day and not even the sound of removal vans would wake him up.”

“Sorry, I don’t quite understand?” She asked.

"Where I live, people are always moving in and out all the time – you'd be amazed how they crash about without a care at all hours. One of these and I snooze through the lot and then up again in the morning bright eyed and bushy-tailed."

"I see…" The woman looked doubtfully at his damp jacket and shirt. She considered the pills in her hand and the man who had given them to her, clearly still uncertain that she had grasped what the Adjuster was telling her clearly.

"To my shame I once gave one to a man that harassed me. It sounds odd I know - but hostels can be strange places. I picked up my things in the night and was gone. He never stood a chance of noticing me. I was free of him and nobody was any the wiser. Perfect. The only problem was finding a place where he would never be able to find me. Could you think of a place you'd never be found? It's not as easy as it sounds."

"I'd have to think about it a bit. But, yes, I suppose I could." She sounded more certain now. There was a note of relief in her voice.

He held out the little package with its silvery top and after a brief hesitation she took them from him.

"Fatigue is a terrible thing to live with… almost as terrible as fear." He noted.

"It is." She looked at the pills in their snug sarcophagi. "I'll come and see you again after a good night's rest. If I need any more of these would you have some?"

"I'm afraid that's all I've got I think. Let me look in the rest of these drawers, no, no need I remember now, that's all there is and if I'm honest I'm not sure it would be right for me to give you more than two. Two means sleep, two means a door kept ajar in the night. Three or more could be, well, something other than sleep. Look at that though: only a few drawers left with anything in them – and when they are all empty, all used for a good purpose: I'll go home. Not the hostel but properly home."

"And where's home for you?" She asked.

"Nearby, I suppose, although I can't recall precisely. I'm sure it will come to me when I set off."

The day grew bleak after she had gone. Even in a light shower that came during the afternoon the Adjuster stared across the roofs of the market, past their faded, candy-stripe rooftops into some far nothingness - oblivious to the wet, the stink of used fat in the air and the dying of the sun.

The food stalls had closed, the remaining vendors were preparing to close their shutters; bringing in the racks of denim jeans and combat trousers, watch straps, workman's coveralls, lighters and boot laces. As the city clock struck five a woman in a heavy gray coat emerged from the covered alleys and picked her way through the butchers and belt-makers. She ducked to avoid the hanging vacuum parts and mobile phone covers. Soon she stood directly in front of the seated Adjuster.

"Look at you. Your jacket is all damp."

She brushed a little water from his shoulder.

"Has anyone come to see you today? It was busy in the surgery. That new doctor I told you about, Dr Anomie. He's been keeping all the patients waiting again. What else? There's a new girl doing the filing, she seems nice, fresh from the temp agency. I spoke to Lucy again to see if she wanted to come up and see you but she finds it a bit weird. I think it scares her."

The glasses adjuster looked across the striped canopy of the market oblivious to her presence.

"Well y'know I told her you hadn't really changed. You're still the same nice guy that gave me a job. I tried telling her it's just shock really. Shock that hasn't worn off. When that boy didn't wake up you just sat down – in shock y' know – nobody could believe he'd gone under and wouldn't just come back. It shocked me. Suppose that's why I'm here too really." She waved her hand in front of his eyes. "It hasn't worn off for me either, not while you're just sitting here putting peoples' glasses back together."

She leaned in close to adjust the lapels on his jacket then straightened his hair a little with her fingers. The Adjuster didn't move a muscle.

"I always hope that in the back of your mind you know you've seen me, that you can remember us all. I brought a few things for your box. God knows what you do with them. It's just odds and ends from work and home - a few things that I saw in that charity shop on the high street." She opened the little drawers until she found the empty ones and dropped something into each.

"The weather's changing." He muttered. The girl looked up at the sky.

"I think you're right." She said and kissed him on the cheek although he gazed without any recognition of his presence at the clouds. She shouldered her bag and left him.

The food stalls had closed, the remaining vendors were preparing to close their shutters; bringing in the racks of denim jeans and combat trousers, watch straps, workman's coveralls, lighters and boot laces. The great city clock struck five and the adjuster stood up and stretched out his arms – the suit jacket rumbling above his shoulders as he shook out the kinks of the day.

“Two today.” He said to himself. “There haven’t been two in a single day since…” he stared into the sky above him and then down at his shoes, “…nearly two weeks ago. Assuming that this really is Tuesday and that day was,” he scanned up and down the back of the market for the imagined footprints of the people he had served, “a Thursday.”

Small brass clasps secured an inlaid panel onto the teak chest, hiding the drawers and making it a smooth continuous box with just two thick leather bands to help carry it. He bent down to find one of the straps for the cabinet and started to lever the heavy object up and onto his back. The Adjuster froze with the box only half on his back, allowing it to slowly slide back down onto the floor. He took two steps back from the cube as if were dangerous.

He got down on his knee and reached forward to unlock the panel, he put that aside and reached for one of the tiny drawers: the very same drawer that had housed the jade elephant earlier that morning. He fumbled at the gold bell handle on its little chain and pulled the drawer out. Holding the small wooden container with one hand he turned it over into his open palm. A ceramic thimble tumbled out and rested in the bowl of his hand.

“I never moved. All day I never moved.” The Adjuster croaked. He rolled the thimble back into the drawer and slotted it back into it place. Each drawer he checked held a new trinket,

“When is it enough?” He asked.

The Eurofood Drama

The shop was a narrow cavern with its white-lit, glass-doored refrigerators of soft drinks and alcohol on one side and the long serving counter on the other. A hinterland of three aisles were stacked tall with instant noodles, tinned fish, loaves both mundane sliced and large round *pide* flat bread, washing-up liquid bottles, sealed plastic sacks of olives, falafel mix and a small fortress of toilet paper. Humming sinisterly at the rear was an open chiller cabinet with its shelves of cheeses beside tubs of humus and taramasalata. See-through plastic sandwich boxes of stiff white bread holding pale meat slices of unknown provenance stood neatly arrayed across the top shelf.

The long serving counter was almost entirely covered by displays of chocolate bars and chewing gum; this left only a few hand breadths available by the poster-covered window for the transaction of business. Behind that gap the devil bearded and cream-capped shopkeeper watched a smartly dressed black gentleman who stood with his head flung back to read the board of tariffs for phone cards. The card sign was hung on the wall behind the counter - to the side of the altar of cigarettes, aspirin and condoms - in front of a selection of whisky miniatures.

The Turk ignored a girl browsing in the back aisles and focused his judgemental stare along his heavy beak of a nose at the man who had contemplated the board for several minutes now.

"How many minutes do you get for five pounds to Nigeria?" Phonecarder asked.

The Turk slid his finger up to the top of the tariff and simply pointed at where the board stated 'Nigeria £5 – 5 minutes'.

"And how many minutes do you get for fifteen pounds?" Phonecarder pressed on unaware of the deathly stare from the Turk who slid his finger down two rows to where the board said 'Nigeria £15 – 30 minutes'.

"So how many minutes do I get for this twenty pound note I have?"

The Turk's finger wavered up and down the board for a moment before being brought back down.

"35 minutes." The Turk said as the girl in the summer dress flitted from the crisps and nuts section to the tissues and clothes softener.

"How can that be right my friend? Where are the savings that I am entitled to for a larger purchase?" The Nigerian spread his hands in disbelief to the Turk who maintained his placid look of disgust.

"I don't make the cards. Now stand aside while I serve other customers."

The girl had been waiting patiently behind Phonecarder with several items in her arms. At that moment a young man burst through the door in a flurry of jeans and black t-shirt. He pushed the girl back against a food stand. As the Turk started to shout at the youth he pulled out a gruesome looking knife and rammed it through the blue fabric with white flowers and into the girl's midriff.

As he backed away with the knife still in his hand, the girl dropped to the floor, her eyes wide in shock. The attacker closed the door to the shop and flitted back and forth in front of it brandishing the knife periodically and breathing like a steam train. Phonecarder rushed over and knelt beside her, his gaze switched from her unreactive face to down along her dress trying to locate the wound.

"Nobody leaves until she's dead!" The thug shook visibly, the knife point direction flashed from the Turk to Phonecarder. He grabbed the sign on the door and fumbled with it while trying to keep his eyes on his hostages and ensure that the 'closed' notice was the right way round.

The Turk watched Phonecarder attempting to treat the girl, putting his hands onto the spot on her abdomen where the knife had slipped in and out.

"You're a doctor?" he asks.

"A very good doctor." Phonecarder looked up at the pacing youth. "Listen boy - why not go? You've done enough harm."

"Not until I see her bleed out. Not 'til then." The blade quivered as he waved it at Phonecarder. The youth's face flicked between rage and panic, his breath quick and short.

“The boy is incensed.” Phonecarder whispered over his shoulder to the Turk.

“Totally deranged I think.” The Turk agreed.

“Get me a towel and come hold it on the wound.”

The Turk slowly walked around the counter, picking up one of the economically priced pink hand towels from a shelf, all the time watching the boy with the blade to see if he would start forward. He arrived with Phonecarder and got down on his knees to hold the towel on her belly as the doctor directed. The girl looked at them both in a mixture of confusion and fear, as if she didn’t really understand why she was on the floor at all.

“You’re the doctor – shouldn’t you hold the towel?” The Turk asked.

“I’ll speak to him, without surgical attention she’ll… well you understand?”

“You think he won’t stab a doctor too?”

Phonecarder rose to his feet and faced the attacker with his hands spread in a peaceful gesture.

“Why, my friend, would you want such a terrible thing to happen?”

“Shut up – just let her bleed!” The boy ranted.

“This is a most grievous crime but it will be better, much, much better, for you to leave and let us take care of her. Just open the door - go out – go on out.”

“Not until that cheating whore dies.” The young man shouted.

"You can't cheat with a fiancée . I'm so tired of sorting out men. Sorting men out. Tired now and tired of that." She whispered.

"Hold still." The Turk said.

"I've never cheated. Always I am playing the game by the rules, always explaining myself - look where that has got me."

"Hold still you foolish girl." The Turk repeated.

"So this is a matter of the heart then?" Phonecarder asked the angry youth.

"Are you his wife?" The Turk asked the girl.

"No." She replied weakly trying to peer down at the stomach wound without raising her head.

The boy flew into a rage.

"I gave her everything and she just threw it in the gutter, no, in my face, threw it in my face!" He wagged the knife at the girl and the shopkeeper which caused Phonecarder to shrink to one side. The Turk remained unmoved, holding the towel against the girl's stomach.

"Have you two been together long?" He asked.

"Just a month." She replied.

"A month? You shouldn't be at the stabbing each other stage until at least four years of marriage."

"You are funny." She grimaced.

"No. I'm married." He said with no discernable sarcasm.

The doctor seemed to suddenly remember that he had intended to talk the boy out of his frenzy and pulled himself away from the confectionary counter between the crazed youth and the girl on the floor.

"Please keep her still", he muttered to the Turk behind him, "and you, yes you, my friend with the knife, think about what you are doing. You say you love this girl, you say you gave her everything. Let us say you did – "

"I did." The boy spat.

" – we say in Nigeria 'One goat cannot carry another goats tail' meaning I can't know what it's like to be you…"

"I think he's going to try though." The Turk sighed.

"Let's just shut up and wait shall we – till she's gone." The boy said with less conviction than before.

"This is a lot of blood." The Turk muttered to himself.

"I'm sorry." The girl said.

"…so I don't know what it's like to be you. Ok. But won't you be lost when she's gone? That is if you love her so much?" Phonecarder pressed on with his intervention causing the young man to increase his pacing up and down in front of the shop door.

"Yes!" The boy whined painfully. "And don't you see how fucked up that is? Something is hurting you – you get away from it don't you? If you can't get away from it you cut it off – but then there's this thing: you need it and hate it and miss it. Who says that's right? No that's wrong – that's the fucking killer."

"He doesn't understand – I was engaged to the boy." The girl whispered to the Turk.

"Engaged to him?" The shopkeeper asked looking at the over wrought assailant.

"No – the boy he saw me with."

"I never had anything before – didn't value anything I mean – I didn't expect to get anything. That's what I was like, acclimatised to it but then – bam – she turns up and I'm all out of water – I can't think. I just can't think. Suddenly I'm all concerned about what job I've got, what I wear, what people say about me, that I'm not measuring up, that I – fuck it – fuck them – I never knew I was supposed to be getting ready did I? I never knew. It's like – don't you see what it's like?" He strained with thought. "Like suddenly being told football is not important."

"Yes that must be a shock." Phonecarder said with little sincerity.

The Turk looked in astonishment at the girl. The towel and his hands were quite soaked in blood by now.

"This boy appears to be in love with you." He said.

"I know." She replied with shallow breaths. Some of the shocked detachment from reality was wearing off now and she started to process the details of her situation. To her credit she remained calm.

Phonecarder took a chocolate bar from the shelf and offered one to the boy but the lover wasn't listening. The assailant paced back and forth with his head down. Phonecarder carried on talking casually at him.

"At least if I am going to die I won't die hungry." He glanced about him. "It's like being stuffed in an old shoe box in here."

The Nigerian examined the rows of cigarettes and lighters, the headache and indigestion pills. On the other side of the shop the rows of beer cans in the refrigerators queued like faces peering through a window at the scene, a Greek chorus bemoaning the terrible events they witnessed through the lit glass of a perilous chapel.

"Are you really a doctor?" The Turk asked.

"I'll have you know I work for the National Health Service sir."

"That produce isn't paid for by the tax payer you know." The Turk eyed the empty wrapper in Phonecarder's hand.

"I'm dying aren't I?" The girl asked no one in particular.

"Perhaps," whispered the Turk, "we don't know yet. Be quiet, there is a doctor here but he is Nigerian."

"Why did you tell the girl that?" Phonecarder hissed.

"I thought she might be comforted to know a doctor was here."

"But why must you qualify it?"

"It is a sin to lie to the dying." The Turk replied.

"So I am going to die?" She asked.

For a moment everyone's eyes were on the girl's belly where the clotted towel was pressed, each estimated in their own mind, with their own methods the chances of surviving such an injury. The silence seemed to stoke the young lover into action.

“Quiet! All of you shut up! Let’s get it done! Stop holding her - let her bleed out and be gone.” He said.

The Turk peered up at the young man with the knife.

“I’m wondering why you don’t come and put a second hole in her? You see I think it was all fine while the blood was hot and you couldn’t think – but now? How is it now? Frightening? Certainly. All those fiery reasons have cooled now haven’t they? It is difficult to be so certain now isn’t it? Mr NHS come here and take care of this girl.”

Phonecarder got down on his knees beside her.

“Don’t listen to him lady: I am a fine doctor.” He said.

“I know - I heard you were Nigerian.” She said.

“You see she’s deluded.” The Turk noted as he rose to his feet.

“If you have things to do shopkeeper I think you should get on and do them.”

Seeing the shopkeeper swap places with Phonecarder, the boy danced with agitation.

“Stay back and leave her alone!” He threatened.

The Turk stroked his beard and took his time collecting his thoughts in front of the youth. He let the moments drag out while all the time he seemed just about on the verge of announcing something but did not. The shopkeeper contemplated the boy and the knife then the ceiling for a few moments and thoughtfully folded his hands in front of him.

“Now listen. It is clear to me you are genuinely – very actually – in love. Is this right?” He asked.

"How can I be – look at this?" The boy waggled the bloody knife.

"This tells me both that you are poorly read and have no significant elders. *The madness* is a term for love in many countries – most of French law is based on that proposition – lovers stab one another in every opera, drama and poem. You're talking to a Turk about stabbing? Ha! Ask any Turkish man and he'll tell you four stories about his cousins in the mountains. What you've done is very horrid but not very unique."

The Turk's candidness caught the boy off-guard; he even lowered the knife slightly and backed up a step.

"What if it is love then? So what? She'll be dead and I'll want to be. I'm supposed to be the man in the pub or on the terraces – I wasn't supposed to be able to handle this – it's like, ", he fumbled for a comparison, "like putting a 9 volt battery in a 3 volt toy."

"Pah! Wake up boy! You think this is all done and over? Far from it, you did this and so now you've only got three choices left to you …"

"Don't hurt anyone else Peter. Don't hurt yourself." The girl called up from the floor, her complexion losing colour and her voice sounding reedy.

"His name is Peter?" Phonecarder asked her nodding at the boy.

"He just saw us together but he didn't know about it before. It had to be finished, had to be done, and that was the only way. I tried to sort it all out." Her eyes looked less focused now.

"What way?" Phonecarder asked.

"To go with him, let him have what he wanted then he'd break it off and leave us alone. Give him what he'd waited for, he said. I didn't realize how difficult that would be to carry on with afterwards. It's always there: undoable."

"This was an arranged marriage?"

"Yes."

The Turk nodded sagely throughout the conversation from the floor, keeping his eyes firmly fixed on the boy.

"As I was saying… It seems to me young man, that there is so much going on in your head that you don't have time to think about the right thing to do. Let me simplify it for you."

He took the knife. It was very quick and casual - he gripped it with his thumb along the blade and whipped it from the youngsters grasp.

"Now you can only do three things. Go out of the door and run. You could kill yourself – I'll give you the knife back for that one of course. Or you can stay. Try to help and explain yourself to the police. Maybe you write to the girl from jail for a bit."

"What's happening? Can I have water please?" The girl asked.

"The Turk has the knife!" Phonecarder said excitedly.

"Don't hurt him please!" She whispered.

"I'll let you decide boy while we take care of her." He opened the refrigerator door and put the knife next to the milk.

"He's put the knife in with the milk!" Phonecarder squealed.

"I feel thirsty. Can I have milk? If there were only water…" The girl mumbled.

The Turk turned his back on the boy and looked with concern at the girl on his shop floor.

“Now Mr. NHS what can I get for you?” He asked.

“Right… Yes. Call an ambulance, get me any bandages you have, search her purse.”

Without the distraction of the assailant the Nigerian gave his full attention to the girl and the wound. He settled into a state of supreme calm.

“Her purse? What for?” The Turk asked.

“Blood type, donor card, details of next of kin – anything that might be useful.” Phonecarder said.

“Is she dying?” The Turk asked gruffly.

“I very much don’t think so.” The doctor said. He was trying to peek under the blood soaked towel and move away all pieces of the summer dress, he tore it wider open.

“B positive.” The girl whispered.

“That’s very brave of you but we should face the truth head on.” The Turk answered with respect.

“I think she means her blood group is ‘B’ positive. Now please? Phone an ambulance?”

The Turk circled round to the other side of the counter and picked up a phone. The boy stood looking at the knife in the refrigerator and the girl on the floor. Eventually he knelt beside her.

"Don't die." He said.

"I'll try not to." She replied.

Once the emergency services had left and the police had taken their statements, Phonecarder and the Turk were left alone in the shop. They stared down at the black stain on the floor where the girl's blood had been, beside it a galvanized bucket with the lance of a mop resting on it.

"You know I've been thinking about it." The Turk said.

"The boy and the girl?" Phonecarder asked.

"No. The twenty pound phone card. I think the trick is probably to think about the minutes per pound you get for the number of pounds you spend. You know that if you spend five pounds you get five minutes, so that's one minute per pound. You know that if you spend fifteen pounds then you get thirty minutes, so that's two minutes per pound. If you take that the rate of savings to remain the same then for twenty pounds you should get something like…", he rubbed his beard for a moment, "…two and a half minutes per pound, so that's fifty minutes."

Phonecarder looked on his comrade in arms with an expression of wonder; he fumbled in his pockets while the Turk still meditated on the stain on his shop floor. The doctor pulled from his pocket a twenty pound note and proffered it to the Turk like a holy donation.

"It is a mystery therefore", the Turk pronounced, "that they do not make a twenty pound card - it would offer significant value for money."

The Throgmorton Driller

A gang of workmen chewed up the tarmac in the middle of Throgmorton Street. They pneumatically pounded her, then forced her lines apart with bars and worked themselves deeper into poor Throgmorton. I walked along the pavement by the red plastic barricade which separated the public from the brutal assault. The street was a byway in comparison to its connecting cousins and this was why it was singled out for special treatment. Throgmorton was hidden away, less travelled and vulnerable.

I passed a sandwich shop crammed with builders, so many of them in the shop's tight confines that it seemed like a record attempt, every one of them covered immodestly with dirt thrown up from their borings into helpless Throgmorton. Poor Throgmorton.

A white plastic cube hung outside the stone portico of the dentist surgery. I suppose that cube was an abstract version of the medieval tradesman's sign: the pawn-broker has his three golden balls and the tooth-puller a gory hanging molar or a dripping pair of pliers. A light dust covering from the violation of Throgmorton lay on the prickly welcome mat and the door required a hard push to open but then ran away so freely that I appeared to enter the surgery at a sprint.

A single patient leafing through her magazine raised an eye at me and then looked back at the glossy pages. I could only see the top inch of an assistant's head over the tall white counter, judging by the inch's shine and faultless grooming it belonged to a young female assistant. That was my uncertain guess though I have been known to be wrong in these matters.

Drawing closer to the chest-height counter I saw a girl struggling with a spring loaded item. Whatever it was for - dental or clerical purposes - it took some effort and all of her concentration to force a tiny cargo into it.

"Hello I have an appointment at..." I began but she jumped and lost her grip on the payload. We both heard it flip through the air and looked about us. I gestured an apology while stepping back from the counter to look around my feet. She put the still not-fully-seen thing into a draw.

"Sorry, don't worry I'll find it later. What time did you say you had an appointment for?" She asked.

"12.45." I smiled and put my hands up on the high counter, leaning in a little to watch her check the computer. As always, a few moments of paranoia stole over me, a close cousin to the feeling when I pay by credit card in a restaurant: I am afraid I will be refused. Would the pretty bob of hair look back up at me never having heard of my appointment even though she has been so pleasant to me so far, how might she change if she finds I am not a proper customer?

"Take a seat and we'll be right with you." She gets up and heads into the rooms beyond the waiting room. Non-waiting areas: doing rooms. I find myself wishing there was a room between the waiting room and the doing rooms where a man could get his courage up if he has not been to the dentist in a few years. Perhaps many stages of rooms I think as my hands dig in the tightly wadded magazine rack. A tiered transition from waiting to doing: one for each year? Then it strikes me that this is the entire purpose of corridors. In my hands I hold a magazine dedicated to pictures of suits, watches and darkly lit cars but my brain gyrates with a new found love of corridors.

I watched the other patient being called through – how relieved she looked that the waiting was over, actually pleased to be getting into the action rooms. She would hardly understand my love of corridors: she might even believe that buildings are better off without them like those offices with all the walls removed. The magazine was lushly shiny and I became embarrassed when I touched it, feeling the stick and grip of my fingers on its vinyl surface. This was heightened when, on turning the page, I was confronted by a bosomed beauty in a stars and stripes bikini just as the assistant came out to let me know the 'dentist would see me now'.

Acting tactfully and knowing how strong my tendency was to sexualise and frame all situations into a drama, a problem that only recently I had become mature enough to face and tackle, I put the magazine back into the rack and asked if I could leave my overcoat somewhere. The assistant took it from me and hung it on a stand.

"I'm a bit nervous." I said.

"Dr Hitzig is very nice. You'll be fine with her. It's the first door on the right." She assured me.

There was a corridor but not much of one. Just time to straighten the trousers, run my tongue over my teeth again and check for any food which had missed the last four brushings, then begin to perspire lightly from a newly lit furnace in my bowels. Why must it be the first right? Why not the second or third doors that I could see further on? Nervous patients should always be given the third door. I entered the bright white doing room.

Dr Hitzig was occupied with her laptop but flashed a little smile when I peeked in. She was dark haired and wore sky blue scrubs, maybe just a modicum over-weight but she had about her a fearful air of vitality and health.

"Mr Färber, come on in. I was wondering from the name whether I'd be meeting someone from the old country. You're not German though are you?" Her accent was that perfection which some European speakers and most of the Netherlands reach with baffling ease. She pointed to the chair with a smile.

"No I'm afraid not, we've been English for some time now. I don't think we're even sure where we originally came from." My stomach tensed as I lay there prone – as if afraid she'd suddenly poke it. I consoled myself by thinking that I had past the point of no return. All that remained now was to open wide and see things through, time would surely pass. Hitzig nodded in an understanding manner and began arranging a paper napkin on my chest.

"I'll just tuck it in." She said and gently hooked the paper into my collar. Hitzig rolled back on her chair to pick up a card from the desk. "It's been a while since you last saw a dentist, is there anything particular you want us to look at?"

"No, nothing's wrong. I've been travelling a lot and haven't had time to the find a dentist until now. The longer I left it the more I was reluctant to get booked in – well anyhow – here I am now. I think I'm going to need a bit of a clean-up." I said trying to find somewhere comfortable to lay my hands that didn't look like I was cupping myself.

"Oh excellent - I hate the boring appointments. Let's get you sorted out." She popped the card back on her desk and quickly shut the lid of the laptop. Conspiratorially she leant in and said, "I've been looking at holidays, I know it's not very professional in the surgery, but this firm looks like a really good one."

She donned a clear plastic face shield and, I had to hand it to her, she somehow made it look the most natural thing in the world like a model donning a new hat. While she began to probe and mirror and press inside my mouth she carried on talking about her current fascination.

"This company does it all. It's not cheap but the destinations are really nice, like say, island cabins that are far from the madding crowds and jungle top lodges, this sort of thing you know?" I made an 'O you don't say' noise around her fingers while trying not to raise my tongue in the way of her ministrations.

She rolled around and got the sucking hose into my mouth then started drilling to her heart's content. I struggled through the acute vibration phase which was followed by a period of saliva pooling that induced gagging and irrepressible tensing of the neck, spine and hands. I tried to think of the islands and the jungle tops she'd described - even of long beautiful corridors that I have known – one from long ago at university that was up lit with glass blocks in the floor. Time couldn't cease to pass entirely could it? Perceived time is t to the power of pain. $\rho = t^P$ where I have used the Greek 'rho' to represent perceived time to distinguish it from P for pain and is coincidently similar to the sound of my struggles with a mouthful of rubber fingers.

Eventually Hitzig got me to sit up and rinse the broken tile fragments from my mouth. I watched carefully to see if I could spot them in the pink fluid that ran around and down the little white sink.

"It's mostly professionals that go. It looks really nicely organised and it's all for singles. They're all about having sex these holidays though aren't they?" Could she have really said this to me so nonchalantly? I didn't doubt it was true –she dabbed some paste onto her polishing drill as if she hadn't just mentioned she was thinking about booking a sexual adventure playground holiday. Her question must have been fully rhetorical as she ploughed in with the buffing, a distinct look of gratification playing on her face. I imagined she drew tremendous satisfaction from the transformation inside my mouth in a few minutes. Was it my oral hygiene that put that look on her face or was it some private vision of carnal pleasure on a desert beach.

Owls do not really see people. Their minds are tuned to only two wavelengths: food and scenery. A human simply gets lumped in the everything-else category. In a similar fashion my inner Englishman discarded the comment, which couldn't possibly exist in this context, as garbled data. As a shy person once almost said, when you have eliminated the indecent, whatever remains, however improbable, must be the truth.

Polishing was a far more pleasant experience, each tooth felt like a little pearl against my tongue. Once more I hit the pink rinse with gusto, now acclimatised to the sarsaparilla-esque taste. I began to wonder how it might taste with a little spiced rum.

"Now let's talk about how you are brushing." Hitzig rattled in a drawer and brought out a lifelike model complete with gums and perfect teeth. She put aside the top set and twirled a toothbrush expertly in her other hand like a poker player rifling his chips. "You need to really get into the gum line at an angle with the brush, you see? This is why you're getting such a build up of plaque here. Do you floss?"

Did I floss? Does rice grow on the moon? Did Thatcher say 'I'll give this one a miss' when she was cutting free milk in schools? No (but maybe she should of, heartless cow).

"Do you have an electric toothbrush?" Hitzig was on a roll now. I shook my head shamefully. "We sell them here you know – these companies give them to the practice at a discount. Come through I'll show you." She led me through the corridor into the waiting room cum reception. There was a distinct feeling in the air that this ordeal was nearly over. She got the assistant to pass her a hybrid between a toothbrush and light sabre.

"This is a really good one – it'll get into those hard to reach places and do all the work for you." The receptionist and I listened patiently knowing that from my vastly lower moral ground I would be buying whatever she told me to buy.

"It's a girl's best friend." She said with a wink.

Hitzig put the toothbrush on the counter and walked with rhythm back into her office. The receptionist and I continued to blink at the spot where she had stood. The inner Englishman struggled to cope, overloaded and admitted defeat. How many reinterpretations of 'girl's best friend' can there be while holding a fast vibrating device in one hand?

"Did you want to take the toothbrush now?" The girl asked in a disbelieving tone.

"Yes. Yes please. Can I have floss and, well I may as well have some - what's its name? Sorry brain like a sieve. Mouthwash! Can I have some mouthwash too please?" I said. I said all those words.

I gave her my credit card without suffering the bout of nervous paranoia. The concern that the money club might suddenly decide to eject me from their community was displaced by a party of thoughts busy redecorating the inside of my head.

I punched in the digits of my PIN: an indignant 5, an excited little 7, a wide-eyed 1 and a wiser, rounder 8. In the back of my mind was the suspicion that you could be thrown in jail for behaving like Hitzig, for really being sexual.

The receptionist gave me my receipt and my bag full of dental goodies. My new life of oral sanctity and moral turpitude was just beginning as I walked out onto Throgmorton Street where men in yellow hard hats were being swallowed up to their necks by a crevasse in the street. In twos and threes those men went down to work on her and Throgmorton just chewed them up and sent them back spent.

The Lift

From the upstairs library of the main building there total 415 paces required to exit the front gates and walk out onto the Strand however using a little known lift PKV could reduce that number to 187. That's a total saving of 228 steps: it only demands he ignore the words cut into the steel above the up and down buttons reading 'Staff Use Only'.

This is the story of how PKV came to lose over one hundred and fourteen pounds in five weeks and then met Patricia at a counselling session - the woman who would go on to become the force behind the man. This is the history of the causes of those happy results. But there I go, opening portholes to the future, some of which are far beyond my right to open, so for now let's consider the very recent past. Twenty minutes should suffice, before Paul Kelvin Vaughn pushes the button.

Picture the lovable, spherical fellow back in the theology library: squeezed against a desk with the sun streaming down from an old leaded window. His trappings on the table but not scattered randomly about. Not PKV's beloved tools. The pencils are slotted into a bamboo tube: this lightweight travel version skips the specialist rods such as the controversial 7H or the bloating 3B and even with these meager rations PKV is capable of producing Blake reproductions, botanical diagrams or, when the occasion calls for it, the odd portrait.

In an angled black lacquer rest next to a bottle of Indian ink rests a Nakaya Japanese fountain pen and two technical drawing pens. PKV's pudgy hand hovers lightly over the fountain pen: his eyes scan the lines of an open book. To the right and left of this manuscript are open notebooks, one of long hand notes in bookkeeper's script and the other a part-formed numerical index. In all my sweet days on earth I never saw anyone who could study as hard as PKV.

Let us take a snapshot view of PKV himself at this point. Over the back of his chair is a smart tweedy jacket, not new, or by any stretch of the imagination a 'fashion jacket'. He wears a white shirt, one tail of which has nearly escaped from his trousers. His leg wear is of a non-descript nature as if to divert attention with blandness away from the capacious buttocks. Notice that PKV himself is relatively broad shouldered, in fact, were it not for two dozen kilos he might pass for a Richard Burton type. His forehead glints with beads of sweat in the sunlight and resembling Burton playing the defrocked minister on a Mexican tour bus in *Night of the Iguana.*

Around the wrist of the outstretched arm PKV prefers the bulkier double cuff requiring the use of cufflinks. Sadly he has mislaid or completely lost the required accessories and bravely improvised with buttons and thread. If we changed PKV into a Camden fashionista - these cufflinks with their quirky eccentricity would be the sole item to remain unchanged.

If we allow a few seconds to flow on the great hand picks up the Nakaya, the lid is removed with perfectly thoughtless practice and placed by the ink bottle. '*In Shinto the well-being of the people is connected to nature, they are given a husbandry role over the islands by the Kami. The patterns of the wounded king or Bran with his cauldron in their relation to the land are comparable, literally co-parables. In this permutation of the quest, king and grail relations, the quest is the first and overarching principle. Care for the land is the imperative.*' His writing is unrushed, the lines composed in his mind before touching the paper, leaving time to enjoy the pleasure of looping, curling and punctuating.

Let us indulge our flexibility in time and hold the moment still before PKV flips the page. We see that above the study notes there is a remark at the top of the page: '*the scarlet sage is pollinated only by the humming bird and its cultivar is known as the snow nymph'*, with lines ruled above and below to distinguish it as an outcrop, a passing notion that has taken PKV's fancy. He doesn't know yet that the idea of a cultivar - a naturally occurring form that is artificially reformed into something new or sublimated - will be the central ideal of his life in eighteen minutes time and from then until he passes out of this veil of tears.

PKV moves across to annotate the left notebook. He marks numbers in the margin, shorthand symbols and punctuation. A study system is at play but it is unclear whether for efficiency or secrecy or both. When he finishes he looks at the blank wall in front of him. The day's work is done. Another topic has been mastered. He appears to be meditating but really his mind is just stepping down from high gear. Perhaps this is what meditation really is? I was never a fan myself.

He lifts a bulky case onto the desk. It looks like the classic doctor's bag and opens the wide mouth to let him move his precious tools inside. He puts the Nakaya in his breast pocket and tucks a heavy library book under his arm. When he squeezes his bulk out from between the chair and desk he finds he is blocking the path of a trolley laden with books driven by an oriental girl. PKV smiles.

"Ah, nowhere to go. Ah. Sorry Anna. How goes the good fight against disorder?" He asks.

"Mighty well thanks." Her American drawl coming complete with a cheeky smile. "I meant to tell you PK, I've been through the stacks again and there are more of those Onaka correspondence boxes missing from the catalogue. They were hiding in French literature." She pronounced his name 'pee-khay' missing the V for additional familiarity. "You'll find them marked with those itsy red recovery stickers."

"O good lord, really? Anna how can I ever repay you? This doctorate is going to be more yours than mine." He backs a few paces up to where he can duck out of her way between two rows. "I suppose it's too much to ask if there were there any photographs, or better still a sketch?"

"Not that I saw – I wasn't fixing to look thoroughly though. There's a Cockerell letter in there though."

"Sydney?" He asked.

"O yea, he gets everywhere. Probably talked Onaka into sending him his favourite brush or yo' know maybe the *Sparrow on the Branch*."

"Somehow I find it difficult to imagine Cockerell and Onaka getting on. Onaka's more likely to have sent him a petal in an envelope - but you never can tell – the old bastard could be fairly persuasive."

She started to push the book cart along again slowly with a thoughtful look on her face.

"See you around the block then." She said as she passed him with a wink.

From our standpoint we see this as an open invitation for further banter but of course at this time I am holding him back. I make it impossible for him to follow her around the corner and squeeze past the cart and ask her out to dance or a bar or goodness knows where. How should I know where? I've no experience of such things. With me gripped around him and holding him in suspension it isn't possible.

PKV has acclimatised to this state of lost opportunities and takes a moment to adjust his shirt then pick up his books and bag. Let us not be downhearted on his behalf as we know that change is literally just around the corner.

With an unmusical form of humming he examines the shelves to find the empty slot for his book to be returned to. After he puts the book back he carefully lines up all the spines so that they are flush with the shelf. Libraries are a suspended place, hanging in the air all about you is that sense that knowledge is being moth-balled, preserved, dipped and pinned like a butterfly. What they lack is anything being firsthand, all things have been passed down.

He proceeds with a burgeoning gait along the stacks to the side stair, down its few stairs to the library main area. The college has several libraries, fewer than it used to, due to the fashion of centralising. This one smells of wood polish and sits on the third and fourth stories in the back quarter of the giant campus building. At the exit there is the traditional librarian's desk disappointingly manned by a pimply boy rather than the exotic Anna.

PKV bumbles past and out into the black and white checked linoleum corridor. There is a lot of human traffic and his bulk is an annoyance to them. This embarrassment factor is critical in his decision making although with our facility to flick back and forth we still cannot expose the inner workings of the mind, we take our cues from little prompts, a rubbing of hands or quickness of breath, but we can never examine at leisure the state of a mind.

Our rotund hero slips into a side corridor with bulletin boards and plain duck egg blue doors with each denizen's name on a strip of plastic and slid into mounted holders, the lack of permanency is at odds with the grand old library. A staff picture board reveals that we are in a wing of the biology department. PKV jauntily corners again at the next intersection and now there is absolutely no one around, even though he has only walked a few dozen paces from the jet stream of students. No ceiling tiles cover the pipes and conduits, all sound and vision seem to be pulled along to the disappearing point at the corridor's far end.

He takes a few bold strides towards the dull burnished steel lift doors that stand proudly where the layout of doors skips a beat. *Staff Use Only.* This is one of those times where a person needs to actively pretend, you need to fake having not done – most especially not seen - something. But of course that's like a flip of quantum physics: what is observed is changed or rather: what is observed will change you but in this case you simply must not let it show. What would dear Stanislavsky say about this, perhaps try to remember a time when one was not perpetrating a miniature by-law crime and act through that? Implausible and also irrelevant: as PKV is as far from a trained actor as we could find. He pushes the down button with raised eyebrows and an inaudible 'oh' on his lips. The button lights up. He dances a little on his toes while his eyes are fixed on the beady, glowing downward triangle.

A ping signals the arrival of the elevator. There are no signs of life along the corridor in either direction. This is a desolate section of the academiverse. The doors slide apart and he slips inside, prodding the ground floor button several times over in the hopes of closing the doors all the quicker. Then he notices that the button below is lit. The 'B1' is lit.

And then he realises he is not alone.

With a rictus smile he turns his neck on a clockwork mechanism. A thin youth in a white coat is there – he must barely be nineteen - one hand leans on a dolly with a white sheet cover. The lift begins to descend again. It is as slow as a cargo lift. The youth gives him a nod.

PKV and the stranger are now locked in. Though he wants to, he can't take his eyes off the student or the cart. He feels he wants to look up to the ceiling or the monstrously slow rotating number above the doors but can't make it happen. The human body is paralysed when it dreams, which is why there are so many dreams about helplessness. I think perhaps PKV involuntarily entered this state but I cannot swear to it. Dream time is as good a description of where I exist now as any.

This is one of those moments where something moribund needs to be said to break the ice, where a skilled societal would comment on the weather or current affairs. But I have been around him for too long, my great mass bound up about him in combination with his freakish study habit. We've made him somewhat unfit for small talk with straightforward humans.

The student's eye line tracks down to the dolly and back to PKV. Impishly I feel. No let's have a closer inspection; the expression is like a curious thought mixed with invitation. It has the essence of game show host blurred with prankster and a hint of indecision. PKV's weight is pushing back against the wall of the elevator. His grip on the handle of his case is tight but the polite expression on his face is forced to stay put, it could well be misconstrued with polite invitation.

Leaning slightly over the trolley the boy gathers a corner of the sheet in his hand. He pulls it back a little and reveals the chrome legs of the dolly, then a little more showing an aluminum edge. Our weight, his and mine, trembles against the wall. Like a magician the boy flips the rest of the sheet back.

He unveils the face of a cadaver considerably far through the process of dissection. On one half the cheek and eye are missing, the ear is a truncated hole, no skin remains, sinews are free with muscles pared and open for investigation. The other half is quite complete, a person with a lone blue eye staring up, aghast, to the ceiling of the lift.

PKV and I share something in this moment - looking carefully at it this time round I feel a good deal more objective – we share an extraordinary cross product between the poetry of anatomy and fear. Forgive me if I revel in it, this is the last minute that we were really still bound together. From this moment on we split like four day old milk, so he could go on and be what he always should have been without me holding him back. And I? I began my journey to the place where the lost things live; all the shapes of branches that have been burnt, the results of failed hypotheses, the patterns in children's broken kaleidoscopes and the fat of a man terrified by a vision of mortality.

We view the ramus of the mandible, through the sphenoid, up to the supraorbital foramen – all syphoning a lake of dread that wells up in the cavity of our chest. The mental protuberance and tuberosities of the chin jut out accusingly, the maxillae in the centre of the face barely holding together, the keystones of the skull underline the critical, unavoidable truth that life: no matter how undefinable, holds the body together and as it leaves, as its glow fades, the body simply dismantles. Without that animating power the body fragments quietly into its component parts.

The kid flips the sheet back over the body. It had been exposed for no more than a handful of seconds.

Now there are different schools of thought on the effect of special revelation on the character of the revelated one. Most popular is the thinking that even though you may have been treated to a divine insight you are still the same, only facets of your character that relate directly to the key fact that has just been communicated will change - if you were lazy before - you'll still be a sloth. This hypothesis helps with some terrible encumbrances on the newly converted Christian, Muslim, Buddhist or popular science reader. Now that you've been struck by the Damascus beam of light you expect to be free of drink, lust, bad breath, midnight snacking, tardiness, anger, bitterness, jealousy and generally making an idiot of yourself. Generally this isn't so. You may be more driven to stop yourself from imbibing or nit-picking – but you still very much want to.

Why should this be so? Isn't the big bad truth enough? Maybe changing the core of you isn't the point of the thunderbolt: maybe it's a more intellectual exercise.

Not in PKVs case. The doctor's bag drops from his hands, he screams and is trying to force the two doors apart to allow his bulk through as fast as possible. When the bag hits the floor it disgorges notebooks, pens and ink bottles onto the metal floor. The medical student tries to calm him but PKD is a whirling dervish, switching between pummeling the buttons with his fist and jamming fingers into the incompliant crack between the doors.

He skids on the Nakamaya and stumbling, crashes backward, sending the student falling to the floor and while desperately flailing with his arms he pulls the sheet back off the cadaver. More screams ensue.

When the lift arrives at the ground floor only seconds later an unfortunate crowd are grouped in the busy foyer with their backs to it. Like a cannon ball through tissue paper PKD decimates the unsuspecting young hipsters, the provocative skirt wearer, the metal heads, the waist-coated dandies, the frocked (for choir), the staring-lost-at-the-building-map and even trammels the odd tutor. All in the imperative requirement: a straight-line need to get out.

We watch him from where he leaves me, through the doors in a box descending to the place of the dead in the basement. Never again will he avoid exercise, nevermore enjoy the little known fifth meal of the day. If not the actual fat then the spirit of the fat of the man – me - has been ejected forcefully.

This is not revelation: this is a rupture. This explains why the effects, and my exile to limbo, are so very upsettingly permanent. So our story must end because I cannot take you any further in time and I must be happy peeking in and around the period when PKD and I were one.

She held up a roll of money to the wind and rubbed her fingers together gently as if she were sowing seeds in the air. The notes zipped out from her fingers and tumbled over and over across the furrows of an arable field. Hundreds of strips dawdled amongst the budding crops until they were ambushed by the breeze and then forced to dance a whirling jig.

Erica got down from the two bar fence and stood in the long grass at the verge of the road. Across the tarmac was a junction leading up to a weighty building on a hill, a white on blue sign read *Hafbourn Hospital.* Erica removed her shoes and put them on the grass as a car passed and the rush of air coiled her hair around her face. She laughed and dabbed her feet onto the rough bitumen, taking each step like a child navigating rock pools, slow and dainty, picking up her knees and pointing her toes gently down.

On the other side she transferred to the pavement where the hospital approach was lined with beech trees, she weaved in and out of them. As she walked she smoothed her hand around the green-grey dusty trunks. The hospital was a turreted maze of yellow bricks and red lintels. On the steps was a young man. Spotting her he put out a cigarette and walked towards her.

"Erica where were you? We were worried."

"That's nice - I wish I could worry." She replied.

In a dark alley she stood drenched and waited patiently. From a window above came the sound of Tony Bennett singing 'The Way You Look Tonight'. A figure comes to her with a blanket and wraps it around her shoulders. Then hands on her shoulders guide her around the corner and into a door.

She was soon in a dormitory where she passed along two lines of beds, each with a warm mound buried in it. The air smelt of old heating system and she sat on a bed in the corner listening to the sleepers shuffle and cough while the radiators tinged and shuddered at regular intervals.

Erica waited for the traffic on the road outside to become silent. She waited until the deep of the night, the verge of the sky changed back from black to grey, until the street lights turned themselves off, until dew formed on the windows, until the first rattle of a lorry and the birds hesitantly started to call out to each other. When she was sure the night had passed and she had dutifully watched it, she laid her head on the pillow and closed her eyes.

"You must sign on." He said. "This way we can get you registered for the hostel and help get you set up." She nodded because she felt this would please the handsome young man. It did. This creature was so different from the people she had spent the night with, she wondered if she peeled away all the rags and faces and tears from those shambles would they all be like this fresh river stream of a boy?

Erica followed another helpful person through the doors, out into the streets, along paths and into a job centre.

"So what can you do?"

"I can sort, fetch, walk, carry and wait. I can manage."

"Ah, clerical work - and management - really? Well maybe we'll see about that later, there's plenty of office work around at the moment - in fact," he rustled with a pile of index cards until he found the one he was looking for, "can you be at an interview tomorrow?"

"Yes. I could be anywhere tomorrow."

"That's good, that's a good attitude. If you can keep an open mind about where and what you might do I think we'll pretty much guarantee to get you something in the next week or two."

He wrote some details onto a card and passed it to her. "This position is only a little way down the road from here, a nice place. They help a lot of people get a new beginning. It's nothing to be ashamed of you know: needing a fresh start."

"I could do with a fresh start. I like the sound of that. Frr-esh start."

She enjoyed the feel of flicking the appointment card with her fingers while the assistant gave her advice about what to say at that nice place. She smiled her universal smile at him and hoped that his words, slipping like silver fish past her, were not too important to him. She riffled the appointment card over her knuckles and then brushed it across her lips while she looked intently at his face. He was very symmetrical, very tidy.

"I'll go and get some sleep." She said.

"A good idea, you'll want to be rested for tomorrow."

In the hostel she strode back through the faces of the missing, back to the bed in the corner. She lay down to wait for the fresh start and for time to begin, where one meaningful thing would pass after another and sense could be made of the cosmos. She held up her hand in front of her face and examined the knuckles, the white moons of the quick of the nails and little webs between each finger. She peered at them closely with patience, turning her hand this way and that. On the back of her hand was a tattoo, no bigger than child's clothing label, in blue ink it said: *Erica Morrow*.

She repeated the words over and over under her breath, quickly then slowly, peaking and dipping, flat and long. She smelt the musty tips of her fingers. *Erica Morrow. Erica Morrow.*

An old man built of frayed suits tied with string lowered himself down on to the bed next to her until he sat with his hands on his knees and looked at her. His face seemed compressed onto one side as if the teeth from the right side of his mouth had been pulled out or lost. His lips were fat and pushed out on one side and then tapered to two thin, squeezed lines on the other, his eye on that side was almost closed and on his head he wore a dirty flat cap pointed - as if by slippage - down his cheek. He grunted and loosened the rope holding several layers of trousers and jackets at the waist.

Reaching over he took the appointment card from the bed side table. His good eye widened to read the words on it and then replaced it on the counter.

"You dunt have to gew to those if you dunt want to." His speech spilled out of the wide side of his mouth. "Dunt feel you have to. Theres some gud jobs, yea, but a lot of them are like gewing to prison."

He looked around at the few people shuffling into the dormitory.

"They arent gewing to just offer the gud ones to someone on charity are thay? Thas no ordinary prison either. Thas made o all the owther prisoners. Look te what i say gal, you cant tell where it ends or how te get out."

She smiled at him from where she lay on the bed and considered his crumpled features. The man of rags and sackcloth lifted the blankets and rolled into bed fully clothed. He lay there with his flat cap still on his head.

“All im saying is you dunt have to gew if you dunt want to.” And with that he closed his eyes and rumbled with some heavy breaths.

Water bubbled up through the center of the great upside-down bottle. Each time someone filled a little paper cone with water the gargle blopped and chogged its way up the glass jar. The bubbles helped her to mark time, the chimes of a drowned clock, and reminded her that she was waiting. She was waiting for something significant.

Erica sat motionless on the overly warm commercial furniture. Her legs were wrapped in an unfamiliar way by a skirt, picked out for her and freshly laundered by someone at the hostel. Two other people waited with her, a man and a woman. The man was flicking through a magazine while the woman read laboriously through some sheets of paper. Erika watched each event that happened in the reception with extra care: seeing if there was any special significance to be gleaned from them. What could be made of the machete-like teeth of the woman behind the desk? What about the bicycle courier whose comedic calves were too large, why did he leave them exposed by his Campari cycling trousers? She waited for revelation to strike.

“Miss Morrow?” The beaver-faced lady behind the desk called out even though she was already looking straight at Erica. “Just down to the left please, first door, they are ready to see you.”

She stood up, which was pleasant after sitting immobile on the faux material for so long. Erika looked in the direction that the receptionist’s arm was pointing and followed it along. She managed a quick ‘thank you’ to the signal hand as she passed, as if floating by on the current of a river. The first entrance she came to had one door pinned open with several reams of A4 paper. It looked inviting, as welcoming an office door as the sirens of Greek myth might ever produce - if they were inclined toward commercial work.

Entering the room a wonderful chrome framed chair was placed in the very center of the room. This was an improvement on the sticky seat in the reception. It shone brightly in the daylight from the windows. She felt it wanted her to sit down on it, in fact she was sure.

“Take a seat please.”

The voice came from figures seated behind a table. They were looking at the marvelous chair too. Erika took her place on it and for a moment felt a touch of leverage on reality. Was that the way it would be, like a bolt of lightning? One moment divorced from the world of meaning and people and language – then like a sky diver whose chute failed to open plunged deep into the other side? But then it passed. She reminded herself to remain vigilant.

Erika looked at the poor shapes hidden behind the table, pushed back from the radiant center. An answer might be close she thought. This did seem like an annunciation.

"Hello Erika. I'm Susan Lodge the human resources director - and this is Peter Philips from team services. Then, on my other side, here is Humbert Coe - he's one of our technical support people. Would you mind if I start by asking you some general questions about yourself? Then we'll get down to letting you hard sell yourself and tell us what you can do for us, ok?"

Erika leaned forward to be sure that the grey chorus were looking at her from beyond the dim.

"Questions about me? Please, ask me anything."

"What do you want Erika? What makes you tick? Tell us, in as few words as you can, what drives you most?" The HR director asked.

Erika shuffled forward in her seat.

"What do I want? I want to be part of a group that understands each other. I want to share in the lives of the people that I'm with, to comprehend them and work together." She paused. "If it's required that I be tested and have to work hard or be patient to get there: I'm willing to do that. Fundamentally I want to connect in a real way, in a meaningful way, with others."

There were a few seconds of silence after she finished then a surprised cough from one of the grey chorus.

"That's quite an aspiration. I like to think that we at VCT provide that kind of nurturing environment, very impressively presented too. We hear a lot of pat answers to interview questions, you know? It's refreshing to get something from the heart. Let's move it up a gear then – Peter do you want to follow up on some of Erikas' ambitions?" The centre silhouette turned to the figure on its left.

"Yes, of course yes." The speaker made a slight teeth-sucking noise. "Very inspiring. Yes, well teams are founded on communication, as you say, communication is so important."

"So important." Echoed the shade on the right.

"Exactly." Peter-from-team-services continued. "To be in a team is more than just to be in a group isn't it? It requires communication, as you say, and the quality of that communication to be…" Peter-from-team-services seemed to feel he had at last found the thread of his monologue, "of a very high quality. We look for a high standard of communication in our teams at VCT. Nothing else will do for us here. That's exactly what we need - people with the desire to communicate. Honestly nothing else really matters, or else comes second, or else is of a different importance."

Peter-from-team-services ran out of breath for a second and relied on his escape pod, his ejector seat, the smart bomb of his vocabulary.

"Don't you agree Humbert?"

The right shade seemed to rumble into activity like a volcano burping to life.

"We use all the tools at our disposal to help our groups communicate in the most cutting-edge of manners. Foundation servers, social media, tweeting, video blogging: these are all important elements to a modern company."

The volcanos' companions bleated with agreement at the last statement. The mountain rumbled on in self-satisfaction.

"It isn't simply that we want to keep teams in communication with each other, we want to innovate by bringing diverse groups together. Studies show diversity in corporate sample groups bring about the best possible results. As I'm sure you are aware Erika."

"Aware, yes, I am aware." Erika enthused from her happy position on the seat in the light.

"I'm sure that you are aware that the position you are applying for isn't very senior." The Susan-Lodge shade flipped some papers over on the table in front of her. "But Erika at VCT there are no unimportant jobs: from what we've heard so far I'm surprised you're applying for something at this level. It says here that you have management experience?"

"I can manage." Erika said.

"Well that might set up a promising career future for you here. But would you be happy to start in a lower position? You see what I'm saying? Wouldn't you become frustrated in a junior position?"

The grey figures either side nodded sagely to this comment clearly feeling that perhaps a core weakness had been exposed.

"Waiting is something I am also very good at. I suppose the secret is to understand that no matter how bad the current situation seems if only waiting is required to progress: time is really irrelevant. It's a matter of priority."

The volcano rumbled again.

"Priorities. Excellent. I was going to ask you some technical questions but I think you've really put your finger on it there. We have to prioritise what we want and where we need to go, there's no other way to arrive at a competitive state in a large corporation."

Erika enjoyed sitting in her pool of sunlight answering the questions of the grey shades even a little disappointed when they wanted to stop.

"When will I find out if I'm going to get a fresh start?" She asked.

"Quite right Erika, we won't keep you on tenterhooks. We have several positions to fill but I don't think I'm speaking out of turn to say we'd like you to start as soon as possible." The Susan-Lodge turned to her colleagues to receive their nods. "Could you come in for orientation tomorrow?"

"Tomorrow, yes of course, I could be anywhere tomorrow."

She shook their hands, noting how they were slim and dry or fat and sweaty. Then she left the glorious sunny spot and the shining chrome chair. Orientation: a new perspective on the world is what she would receive tomorrow, if she was only patient.

In one hand Erika held a grey folder which she had been told was the staff handbook and in the other a glistening white mug with the initials VCT printed in large, blue letters on the side.

"This is your desk. Sorry it's the small one but there's only this end of the area left and the full size ones don't fit in between the filing cabinets. We'll see if we can find you a pedestal drawer to go with it, we got the short straw in the last shuffle and I think

Sales cherry picked what they wanted out of the good stuff." Mary gestured with every apology and each one seemed attached to another chapter of the office history. As she waved her arms to point things out, Erika's attention was drawn to the shapeless dress she wore, its large blocks of asymmetric colour in red, yellow and black. A cosmic artist had placed in the open, privacy-deprived area of the office a sculpted, waving Mary-manikin to display the incongruent item to its full potential.

"Sorry about your computer. It'll be set up later in the week. We put the request into the boys last week - they're great laughs. Maybe we'll go and see them to ask when your stuff is coming in." Mary continued unabated. "All these files," she gestured at the long lines of dusty, faded pastel spines, "are left over from the old system and they never got put into the new system. When someone wants to know something about an old case they send a slip through the internal mail with the details." She rustled through her in-tray until she found an orange envelope and extracted a few inches of paper from it. "We go through the files here and find that person and then fill in one of these." She held up a form of several folded sheets. "Then put that back in the envelope to the person who requested it."

From the look of the pile of orange envelopes in her in tray Mary had allowed quite a lot of requests to stagnate. Erica nodded appreciatively. The envelopes were secured by a short tether of string which was spun around two little card discs, one on the body of the envelope and one on the flap. Opening, replying, closing. They go out in the container they arrived in.

Meanwhile the Mary-dress had moved along the faded teal, buff, mute-pink and leavened blue folders on the shelves.

"At the moment you just have to look through all the shelves to find a folder, sorry, they are in age order. Oldest here." She tapped the top file beside her, a drab brown veteran with the name 'R. Wood' written on its spine.

Erika sat at her desk and considered her position. The helpful Kandinsky-dress-Mary had left to talk with a boy in payroll about arranging a pub quiz. She remained alert to any possibility of revelation.

With one hand she unwound the string from an orange envelope, twirling it on and off. A hundred or more sister envelopes were distributed between Mary-the-dress's desk, her own and a pile that been secreted under both desks. She breathed in deeply, feeling that with patience some meaning might form out of the situation. She inhaled like the sea drawing in pebbles. Each request coming in held a slip: each slip held a clue and each clue was to be returned. Add together all the slips, all the clues and what would you get?

She was still considering the matter when Mary-the-dress returned from several hours of socialising with the boys in accounting.

"Five o'clock – time to knock off." She pulled an enormous puffer jacket from the back of her chair. "See you tomorrow at the same time ok?"

Erika nodded and smiled, watching the gorgeous clashing squares of colour bounce their way out of the office. She began mimicking the instructions she had heard earlier. Take an envelope, open it. Take the slip, read the name. Find the name in the folders. Copy out the information. Put the information back in the envelope and send the answer back. Send the answer back.

In the morning another Mary appeared, this one stripped off her puffer jacket and revealed a new puce frock with two large pockets of grassy green sewn onto it. Erika instantly felt that she wanted to put her hands into those pockets, but resisted, as she was still waiting for answers.

"You're here bright an early - sorry I'm late I was out with those tinkers from accounting." Large-pocket-Mary announced.

Mary-of-the-pockets froze as she looked at her desk. She lowered herself slowly onto her seat. Erika's desk was in the same spotless condition with not a trace of a single orange envelope.

"Did you stack all the requests somewhere? It's lovely and tidy but you know they were in order and we're supposed to answer them the same way they came in."

"They were answered in the same order they were stacked." Erika answered patiently.

Large-pocket-Mary looked under the desk. There were no envelopes beneath the desk either. "What about…When?" She stuttered and then noticed some change in character in the walls of folders surrounding them. Her hand pointed limply at the cabinets. "Are they different?"

"Alphabetical." Erika nodded, very pleased that communication, her frequent bugbear, was going so well.

At that moment a young man in his early twenties stumbled around the corner carrying a computer with a screen balanced on top.

"Alright ladies." He said with a smile. "Whose for some new kit?"

Erika watched the man setting up her computer. *Grand-poches*-Mary wandered out of their section of the office as if her night out with accounting had suddenly caught up with her. After a few minutes she returned with a round gentleman who she whispered to and exchanged gestures at the desks and folders with. She and the round fellow then set off to bring back an austere looking woman with whom they repeated the pantomime of whispers and gestures.

Finally the Susan-Lodge appeared and wondered if she could have a word with Erika. She took her new recruit over to the kitchenette where the staff could prepare a dazzling array of instant tea or equally instant coffee.

"Really Erika," she chortled, "I know we sent you down to work with the grass-roots but there was no need to make such an extravagant gesture. You could have come and told me how much time was being wasted on old case information."

"I felt this would result in answers."

Susan-Lodge twiddled the cups laying on the counter so that all the handles faced in the same direction.

"Well you were right of course. A good number of lapsed cases have been brought to light and the expensive business process consultants we hired only six months ago have been contacted to justify themselves – we expect to claw back a considerable sum from their fees. This gives me an unexpected budget increase that I'll need to handle before the end of the year."

"I am sorry." Erika said.

"No need to be sardonic my dear, budgets simply must be spent as we all know or else they decay."

So only a few days later Erika was enjoying the sensation of a large rotating chair in a quiet office of her own. A young man, only just out of university, came in and waited until he had her attention.

"Susan would like to know what you think is the best place for Mary, she thought you would have the most insight."

"Well Mary likes the boys in accounts and thinks the boys in IT are nice. We should give her a job in both."

"Technology budgets? She'll need a lot of retraining."

"It sounds perfect: tech-nology bud-get."

"I'll get the contract to her immediately Erika."

The skinny youth backpedalled out of the office and left her to continue rotating on her chair.

During the remainder of the day Erika made almost twenty more appointments as well as ordering several departments renamed. Which of her radical decisions was the critical final blow was difficult to determine: there was well received institution of a free canteen for staff, paid leave for an entire legal department to go skiing, contracting a group of quantative analysts to determine what 'communication' was, opening a public question and answer centre, commissioning a company theme song, colour-coding the sales force and ordering a series of early morning daily debates.

At a quickly convened meeting of the Susan-Lodge, the volcano and Peter-from-team-services Erika began to despair that her fresh start would truly end in a break through.

“This emergency meeting is to clear up a few background items that have shown up in our checks – we’re certain that all this can be sorted out. It has come to attention that you may have been resident at a mental institution prior to taking up your position with us Erika?”

Erika stared at them with a warm smile, she could feel them trying to understand - to say something really meaningful to her – so she reached out to them with all her heart.

“I was a resident somewhere prior to this. Yes, I think I was definitely somewhere.”

“It says here that you were at the Hafbourn Institute?” Susan-lodge asked.

“Definitely.” Erika said.

“This could be difficult for us Erika,” cut in the volcano, “because although we are clearly supportive of people with mental health needs, we should know how much you really understand of what’s going on - so that we can help you - you see?”

“Understand?” Erika’s expression dropped. “I want to be part of a group that understands me. I want to share in the lives of the people that I’m with, to comprehend them and work together - so far no progress I’m afraid. I stay alert for every word and gesture every change of the weather and the noises from outside.” She got up and began to pace around the three executives then took a place at the window looking out at the bustling world below. “The objects that can talk: I listen to, the things that stand and walk: I follow. But have I never found a shred of meaning, something to explain why any one thing should be where it is. Not in my whole life. I can see everything but I don't really believe it."

Susan-Lodge rose to her feet.

"Erika we are in a position to make an extremely generous cash offering to you."

"Yes - a generous cash offer - you see that sounds lovely – cashhh, cashhh, cA-shh - but what does it mean? Do I want it – who can tell?"

At this point Peter-from-team-services began to openly sob against the table and the volcano wheezed asthmatically toward Erika.

"You'll take the offer though? We have a solicitor ready to counter sign documents and provide the compensation. Now I understand you don't have a bank account so the full sum is ready for you in cash. Be reasonable Erika, our positions are on the line here, maybe the whole company!"

Erika turned and smiled warmly at the three disturbed executives.

“So how did you like the outside world Erika?” The orderly asked.

“It was a terrible experiment I’m afraid Dominic. I don’t know what possessed me to look there for meaning.”

She watched as the man carefully straightened the blankets and sheets on her bed.

“Didn’t you find anything you liked?”

“There was a lovely dress, a wonderful shining chair and fields of money.”

“Fields of money?”

“Well at least one.” She peered out of the window over the trees and main road. “In fact that field there.”

She pointed and the nurse peered out.

“Is that really money?”

“Oh yes, I put it there only a little while ago.”

The orderly stared and stared, trying to make out what the scraps rolling around might be. He then turned slowly on one heel and ran quickly out of the door, never to be seen again at that institution.

The black-haired, eight-eyed face loomed in front of me, a drop of light in each great black ball. I scream soundlessly with a wide open mouth.

Knock it off. She signed with her front two striped limbs then dipped the point of one into an ink bottle and reached over to cross out a section on the paper. I settle down and watch her slicing out the flotsam from the page. She bracketed a large section and noted *confused* in the margin beside it. *Read it back again.* She rested her front legs on the desk, the back four legs and her bulbous abdomen on the floor. I adjusted my glasses and picked up the paper.

"Ahem. We had made no provision for our futures, we the generation X, the post-baby boomers. And now we had to work until we dropped, no retirements, no state provision for ageing. Hands arthritic, we were forced to..."

Change to 'arthritic hands' *– hands arthritic sounds like a poetry reversal.*

I nodded at that sage piece of counsel. We tried to keep the glamour to a minimum and use the unseen elements: tempo, constriction and word palettes. I drew an arrow to indicate the change. Don't think that she was opposed to poetry, quite the opposite, sometimes she would hold back the editor's sword from a passage I felt was over-pushed. She sent off poems to *High Bank* occasionally and at least one had found its way into print.

"...Arthritic hands were forced to be industrious to earn their next meal. It is said that this caused the children of those gray slaves to be even more disillusioned: suddenly deprived of work by a desperate and over-qualified senior generation. Higher education applications dropped to an all-time low and the young reversed into attitudes of nomadic manual labour and the usual heated emotional music."

Heated emotional music. Sounds a bit condescending doesn't it? She had an art for empathy that I lacked with my Camus-like attitude.

"I'm trying to imply that in every generation the youth music is overly emotional. It may be part of the nature of the beast: flappers in the 1920s, punk in the 1970s, Beethoven in the 18th century. This generation didn't break that rule."

If it's a constant to every generation then perhaps it's not relevant as a description of what made that generation different. She tapped a leg tip on the desk to emphasis the final word 'different'. Dit dit dah like Morse code - editor calling writer: listen to me when I tell you something. Shaking my head I sucked air through my teeth, twiddled the pen in my hand and then committed some pride swallowing rework.

"...and the youth reversed into a nomadic existence of manual labour, music and other consolations of a relegated underclass." She put the tips of her first and second legs together to show satisfaction. I got up to put the kettle on, my knees and back cracking. "A little something for you too Madame?" I crack the seal on the fridge and offer a bottle of Coke with flies floating around in it.

No, it'll make me sleepy and I want to get this finished. I shrugged and swapped it for the milk bottle. When the kettle clicked off I ceremoniously drown a teabag. *Sam – do you think this what people really want to read? A historical prelude to the state of affairs? Whatever happened to jumping in at the action, you know, start with the punch - kiss it better later?*

"We put the reader into a state of clarity instead. There's a lot of confusion about how or why somebody ends up discarded but this is *fraction* which really sells at the moment – people feel if you hit them with the story up front you're cheating: it's a trick that's been pulled too many times. Think of it as a descent, down and down to the detail. It's not my favourite but it's one way of doing it. If it makes you feel better, think of it as harking back to Rousseau and those huge chapter headings that tell you everything that happens ahead of time."

She spindled backwards into her favourite corner and tugged on a strand of silk - always a sign that she was introspecting.

Why shouldn't you write something that's heart-warming? Write to create a change in the reader – not fulfil their expectations – write something they pick up and get one of those revelatory moments from?

"O, I see. It's the literature thing you want is it? I thought you were supposed to be the editor on this one - we can change seats you know. I'll rehash as you write if you like." I said.

You're about to tell me that literature is something you write for after the grave aren't you? I nod. *Sorry, I suppose I'm just caught up in the great writing rubbish. You don't really understand because you've already been lauded for* Spectres *but I wasn't there for that. The need is still in me.*

I'd written Spectres in my middle age although inside I still thought I was young at the time. It achieved that most laughable of things: critical success. This means that you can open doors and use it as a pass card to more fiscally rewarding projects: I had the skills to pay the bills. People refer to *Spectres* as one of their favourite books to look intellectual, especially politicians. What my editor never knew was that the follow up book lay in dust - demonized inside the cabinet that she slept above. She did know that I was genuine about the offer to change role, my preciousness over writing had died some thirty years ago along with my ambition to climb the Matterhorn.

No, you write. She signed. *It's better and quicker that way. We need the money don't we?*

How she strung me the merry dance. It was almost like having a wife again. I did what most old people enjoy doing: I offered advice to the young.

"This is about you having children again isn't it? You think if the times we live in change radically then you won't need a gazillion in the bank to find the man you love and lay an egg. O Clara, I really do sympathise. It's a horrible thing but we aren't going to change the world, maybe the next world, but not this one. Have you even met anyone yet?"

Silly old man. There are a thousand corners and dating sites I could go on to meet someone. I'm not as addled by my instincts as you think. Don't confuse my love for Browning with some strange need to have a partner for life. I want the love of a child not a Romeo. She shimmied her v-stripped abdomen in amusement.

“Paying up front for a child’s life is where we are now. If you really don’t care about the father”, she riled as he used the word *father*, “then you should just help me write some cash cows. How much is it we are talking about?” Another elder thing to do is bring the details of money right to the front and embarrass the arse off the youth in question.

Come on - let’s not exchange seats – we both know that will lead to me over-hashing and you losing interest. After all, people don’t want to read a book by me – they want to read the mighty Balfour, his senses unbowed with age, his insight sharp as a cleaver.

If the old love to advise, I thought, then this is the corollary: the young like to hold up a mirror to the reputations of the old, and who can stand up to that?

So we resumed our positions, she monitored me from a half-crouch at the end of the desk. Normally I couldn’t stand that much scrutiny while working but Clara was different. She was inside the creative horizon. I would often stop to see if she had anything to say about the last sentence or phrase and if she was happy she would just nod a little and I’d carry on.

“Mr. Ryley. Thanks for coming.”

“No problem - anything for Roman you know that – it’s just I can only give you thirty minutes as I’ve got to be across town for dinner.”

The doctor held the door open for Ryley who cast an eye about the room. A desk complete with whirring laptop and a grey-haired man typing. The typist didn’t appear to notice either Ryley or the doctor. There was an acrid urine smell in the air. A bed. A TV.

"I'm sorry about that." She led back outside the room to call a nurse. "Just a part of our problem. We've asked you here to help with. As soon as he starts working he loses all sense of himself. He'll soil himself, not eat or sleep – without any apparent discomfort. If we remove the computer he'll become very upset: it's only by chance it's here – it was a previous patients who passed away, he never used so it was folded up in a corner. Well, the nurses heard Mr Balfour was a writer and just assumed it was part of his things."

"I see, and how can I help you?" Ryley asked.

"I feel he's finding comfort in his old work habit. The rest of the world is so confusing to him with his senility at this advanced stage. What I thought is that you might remember old habits he had, part of his daily routine so that we could, if you like, signal to him that it's time for bed or meals."

Ryley undid a button on his jacket and sat down on the hospital bed.

"He was always a strange one, never had a wife. Spent quite a while in Poland each year then would come back to London for the winter, said London was best in winter, and wrote whatever needed writing; only author I ever knew that never needed an extension."

"I was thinking of more personal habits, things we might be able to replicate here at the hospital."

"Tea perhaps? The man drank it on the hour. I don't just mean often, I mean he'd have it at eleven, twelve, one, two, three. I used to arrive at five so he'd be boiling the kettle and I could have a few words without disturbing him in mid flow." Ryley said.

"Anything else? Bedtime rituals?" The doctor asked.

"I doubt anyone can help you on that score." Ryley paused and stared for a moment at the writer. "But they say, don't they, that everyone reveals more than they intend when they write?"

"Do they?" She sounded tired. She stood directly in front of the writer's desk and eyed the laptop with suspicion.

"In *Spectres* the main character is haunted by his past, he can't sleep and the story is told in reflection: a twilight of life spent wishing to sleep and sleep with dreams of a former life. There's the rub."

"I'll just remind you that I haven't read this book."

"You should doctor, you really should, don't be too busy saving lives to spare a little time for the good of your own soul. *Spectres* was described as the greatest act of optimism in the last century. If I remember correctly the unnamed protagonist's son brings him a bottle of Hine brandy because he knows that his father uses it to get to sleep every night."

"I'm not sure that the hospital carries Hine in the gift shop or the pharmacy but we'll see what we can get. Could you call me if anything else occurs to you?"

Ryley watched his client tapping away at the keyboard and said, "I'll do better than that, I'll bring some myself tomorrow. The son watches over him you see doctor, waits for him to cure himself of the past because there is a wedding to go to - but enough spoilers – I don't want to ruin it for you."

"I wouldn't get your hopes up for any recognition."

"Neither does the son."

Ryley rose and buttoned his jacket. At the door he stopped and looked back at the author.

"How long has he been here?" He asked.

"Just a few days."

"And he writes every day?"

"Every day – like clockwork."

"He'll carry on into the night", the doctor whispered, "unless we stop him."

"Let's just let him go on a little longer shall we?" Ryley looked over Balfour's shoulder at the text building on the screen. He read the lines as the oblivious author composed them. The peeping Tom caught his breath and crept back around to the doctor. He gripped her forearm.

"He's writing about Marlow - you see?" The doctor shook her head. "You still haven't read Spectres? Gads woman! Marlow is the character we never get to see – he's only mentioned twice – once as the signatory on a cheque and once in a photograph sitting on top of a piano. You see?" Another head shake. "Balfour is writing the follow up to Spectres."

"But he's senile, he doesn't even pause to think, surely it'll be nonsense." The doctor said.

"His sense of place and time may be addled but from a quick sample it doesn't seemed to have affected his writing at all. In fact, I'd say he seems back to his former glory." Ryley rubbed his chin and looked sidelong at the author tapping at his keyboard.

"I need to speak with you about a very generous offer to pay for his care and any, absolutely any, remedial treatment for his condition." He said.

"Ah, I see. But you'll want access to what he writes I suppose? Even an unconscious patient has rights Mr Ryley – what next? Reselling the fruit left for coma victims?"

"He has no family. He has no will to determine who should control his literary estate – there's just me, his agent, I'm trying to take care of him, don't you see? This way he gets all the attention he needs *in perpetua* and the world gets another masterpiece, your hospital never needs to worry about which flea pit to send him when his bank account runs dry."

"There are questions of consent here."

"Whatever happened to 'do no harm' doctor? Without this book deal Balfour will slip away and rot in some charity hospice – but if his gifts are used wisely – by you, he could live an entirely better life. Balfour never wrote a book that he didn't intend to sell, he was no premadonna, somewhere in the back of his mind he believes this book he's writing is going to be read. What good is it if it's never read doctor?"

"I'm not sure you fully understand the 'no harm' principle, we do our best for the patient without serving ourselves, the hospital or convenience – or indeed literature. My old tutor said 'you treat the great and the ghastly alike'. I'm more suspicious that you are only concerned with a cut of the profits."

"Hey look at least I knew Roman Balfour before this happened to him. I knew him professionally and personally. He was always too polite to mention how I made my money from the back of his hard work, too gentle to push it out into the market the way I did." He paused to remember. "And not a little embarrassed to take money back from me for selling international rights and adaptations to his work, he considered it to be money for doing nothing. All I'm saying is just let me keep on doing that for him – I've got precedent in that – I've done it for him before."

It's the way you move. She said.

"What? Oh this is just too rich." Roman laughed.

No, really, it's not just the muscle thing, all mammals have that kind of smooth and slow thing but humans have that really odd way of gesturing, even looking. Maybe it's silly but it looks like there's too many motions involved and it doesn't seem natural.

"I cannot sit here and try to defend human beings as the world's scariest creature: what about polar bears? Tigers? A great white shark?"

All very dangerous but also escapable: they just don't have that pursuant malice. Look, I'm not trying to be rude Roman but you should know how it feels to be outside the whole human paradigm, I'm just being honest.

"Alright, alright. I guess I should try to act my years. That's fair comment but I think when I was a child we were all hoping for so much more from the future. I had the feeling that under all the crime and war, mankind really was good. I mean really good. Good with a capital 'G'. Without knowing it we were all proud citizens of humanity marching forward. There was a smile on our faces and a spring in our step but by the next generation we'd blown it: the children knew it and we knew it but couldn't admit it. That's why I struggle to think of us as the bad guys – worse than that – the villains. I've still got that little bit of hope left in me."

She put the tips of her second legs together.

Now that's more like it. Put that down in the first chapter, it's got real heart about it, I can sympathize with that. She pointed back to the keyboard.

I started paging back.

You're not a villain Roman. She said.

I scanned backwards through the manuscript. How quickly the young forgive.

"Maybe I am, maybe I'm not. I'm an illusionist by profession. I often feel that I'm trying to lie my way to the truth – does that sound ridiculous?" I looked up at Clara's unreadable eight black eyes then clutched my chest dramatically. "Quick the pills! The old man's having an attack of philosophy! I knew there was something wrong with him ever since he started wearing a beret!"

She twirled her mandibles in the sign form of a chuckle. *You know I don't believe you are cynical as you think. The great Balfour: optimist writer – isn't dead he's just having a crisis of faith. You're thinking about things in a very win or lose fashion; some good things have come out of humanity not getting it quite right. Take me for example. Look why don't I leave you to a few hours of unmonitored writing? We're short on milk aren't we?*

I nodded and watched her as she went round to the window, pried it open and scuttled out.

"You left it open again!" I shouted out of the window and pulled down the sliding pane. Unmonitored writing indeed, by my age you built up so many ghosts in your head – shades of yourself and others – that the chances of free and unmonitored writing were extremely small. I started typing;

...without knowing it we were all proud citizens of humanity...

Reverse engineering humans is not as difficult as you might think; building a body, a meat vessel to put them in is probably far more difficult than you can imagine. And when things are too difficult what do we do? We compromise. I'll take half of paradise right now please. Which bodies are resilient, cheap, numerous and fast growing? Not human bodies – no siree – insect bodies. A wonder of evolutionary design which is still around for very good reasons.

"So you're pregnant?" I asked.

Clara tucked all her legs under herself in shame. She didn't sign a word. Shame. Such a silly emotion, one that is best soonest grown out of. It was shame that got all those young mothers sent away to the countryside, like H.G. Wells' Mistress, where they remained shamefully lonely and shamefully remote. I brought a chair toward her corner and sat slowly down, levering my weight through my hands on my knees.

"How pregnant? I mean how far along are you?" I asked.

At least a week. She signed.

"How many?"

Fifteen. O god Balfour. Fifteen! And I don't have enough money for even one. I can't just let them sterilize them. But if I let them go on – well I can't bear to think of them being born to short lives of suffering. What can I do? I'm scared and embarrassed and frightened. Why is life so cruel?

“Let’s talk about it and see what we can think up eh? I know it seems bleak now but we’ll come up with something. What do other mothers like you do? What are all the possibilities? Maybe there’s somewhere we can go for help?”

My voice was steady. It had the tone of a grandparent or a councillor. I had never had children of my own like many of my generation. I wished now that I’d more experience to draw on.

The clinic will sterilize them of course – kill them – then tell me to come back when I’ve got the funds and then we’ll let your children live. If they hatch untreated there’s only a ten percent chance they will live out the first week and then only for goodness knows how much longer they’d make it. She shuddered. *I couldn’t bear that: watching hopeless things that I’ve made in pain. How can I feel so responsible when I know how irresponsible I’ve been?*

“What about the father? Could he help you?”

No. It’s not in our natures Balfour. Even if he did want to be involved I think he’s on national infrastructure service which means he doesn’t have two pennies to rub together.

I shifted my chair closer and leant forward a bit toward her.

“What about just one? Maybe we can get you some money in advance?” He said softly.

My editor twitched her mandibles, a movement that reminded me of a child chewing its cheek in thought.

Just one? She signed with a weak gesture.

“How effective?” Ryley asked.

"Exceptionally, in the top percentile of the trial, I've a theory that his automatic writing has kept his neurology in an active state like a prisoner exercising in a cell. The brain has been compared to a computer but sometimes it's helpful to think of it as a system of garden hoses."

"I'm unsure where this metaphor is going doctor – this isn't revenge for harassing you about your lack of reading is it?" He said.

"Not at all and I *did* read *Spectres.* Very enlightening - very touching. What I mean is that hoses only really hold up while under pressure from the water flowing inside them and you can think of the mind in a similar way, without information flowing rapidly through it the pipes collapse into a heap and lose its natural arrangement. Our patient has incidentally kept some of that flow circling round even while his condition continued to pinch off the supply of information from the outside world."

"I hope we can rely on you for a quote to the press: 'writing saved my life' has a lovely ring."

"Of course: in fact you can quote directly from the article I've had accepted to the Journal of Neurology if you like."

Ryley blessed the doctor with a grin normally reserved for publishers who had accepted one of his writers.

"Well congratulations! It seems as if everyone has got something out of this. Shall we go and see the source of our unconfined joy then?"

She knocked on the door and waited for a faint 'come in' from the opposite side. Roman was propped up in his bed, a spoon in one hand and a pot of some desert in his other. He looked weary and drawn but clearly with more presence than on Ryley's last visit. In fact by comparison his personality seemed to pervade the room. On the writing desk was the open laptop.

Ryley clapped his chubby hands together in delight and went to Roman to hug him, shake his hand or otherwise express his glee but the spoon and the desert came between them. Both laughed and Ryley kept up a litany of *Well done Roman - Our own Lazarus - Just look at you.*

With a rattle the nurse entered carrying a tray with cups of tea on it and placed it on the table beside the bed. Roman thanked her and invited the doctor and agent to take a seat.

"What was it like then? All that time?" Ryley asked.

"Like missing time. I do remember a glass of brandy or the smell of a glass of brandy very clearly. Other than that I don't have much recollection until I saw the face of the nurse, Ms. Chandrapaul, one morning. Then I recognised that I was looking at someone and that I was in a hospital room then the fog started to clear."

"So nothing at all from the whole time you were writing?" The doctor put in.

"Not a thing." Roman looked sad as he talked. The doctor touched his hand.

"I think I can say you are the most productive coma victim we have ever had. Your physical condition should quickly recover with a little physiotherapy. I don't know if this is any consolation to you but the results from the medical trials you've been involved in over the past year have been a significant contribution to understanding neuron ageing and even cell death in general."

"Don't mind my attitude doctor. I really am very grateful. I never thought I'd ever contribute anything to science, frankly I've always been a bit of a luddite."

There was a pause while they all sipped at their tea. After a little while the agent couldn't hold himself back any longer.

"And have you read it then Roman?"

"I have. Several times now."

"Come on then don't be coy. Tell me what you think."

"It hurts me to say that it's probably better than *Spectres*. A horrible thing to say because as much as I know it was my body that sat at the table and typed it out, it doesn't seem like I wrote it. I haven't got access to the cogs grinding behind the scenes. I don't even know what the title should be."

The writer looked over at the laptop in despair. His manager was not to be so easily subdued.

"A sequel though Roman, a towering sequel!" He enthused.

"It's worse than that – it's as if somebody has written the book I always want to write and has raided all my hidden thoughts and feelings to do it."

The agent stood up and paced around.

"I don't understand you Roman. This process saved your life and let you express all the deepest parts of your creativity - all the skills that you have built up over a lifetime." He pointed his finger at Roman's chest. "Your lifetime. Your skills. It's a direct expression of you. Think of it like this: you were building up a machine for this book and then one night you started the workings and went to sleep. In the morning you find what the machine - your machine - had created. What you have created. Please Roman don't say what I think you are going to."

"It's not my book. I won't publish it. This is not the equivalent of leaving a stew to simmer."

The next words from of his agent's mouth included *ungrateful* and *fuck*.

In a shabby public house just off Novodevichy Crescent I met up with the unkempt, overweight figure from my long distant past and we shook hands. We clasped hands as respected enemies might do long after the days of fighting have past. Ryley looked me up and down as if I was a revenant brought back from the grave which I suppose with my frugal living and undeserved age I must have looked very like.

I put the pod on the bar for him and we both stared at it for a while. It lay there grey and mundane like a beached pebble without a care for our mixed feelings.

"What's brought this on then Balfour?" There didn't seem to be as much accusation in his voice as I had expected. Had I wronged him? It's difficult to recall enough detail for me to be certain.

"Fatherhood." I said.

Ryley stared at me for a moment then roared with laughter and beat the bar with his hand. I let out a grin that welled up inside me. I enjoyed the moment as I doubted there would be many more of them with such poignancy in this life.

"This is the joke that we waited fifty years for the punch line is it Roman? Really? Fatherhood? You know I always thought that someday I would hear that this", he tapped the pebble, "was being published. I braced myself to be cut out of the picture and just spectate while the carnival went on. You know I have a copy of it from the hospital don't you? I thought about shoving it out into the public waters like a Viking longboat."

He looked abashedly at the bare wooden floor boards.

"You don't have a copy of this one Ryley." I said.

"Really Balfour? Have you improved on what your sleeping self deemed perfect?" There was definite bitterness in his voice.

I took up the pebble and put it in his warm, large hand.

"This one has a title."

My tolerance for emotional meetings had come to an end and I made to leave but he stopped me with a hand on my shoulder.

"This pub is one of the few that has Hine brandy behind the bar. Let me buy you one and we'll talk about what I should buy you two as a christening present shall we? Are you married? Do I know the lucky lady?" His tone was warm now and I saw past the years of change to the Ryley who I'd trusted implicitly for the first half of my life in another era.

"I don't think so. She's a poet. We've worked together for a long time now. We're not married at the moment and there are quite a few details to sort out before anything like that can happen."

Two robust glasses arrived on the bar and the air filled with the sweet, warm musk of brandy. My agent picked his up and warmed the schooner with his hands.

"What shall we drink to then? The book?"

I picked up my glass and considered the tawny spirits, this was a pleasure I hadn't smelt or touched in fifty years.

"To large families." I said.

Entroduction

Comedy is the cover for pain: tragedy and comedy operate on a revolving door basis, in this way they are similar to Clarke Kent and Superman but not quite so mutually exclusive.

This anthology is one of weak and easily criticised people like you and I who, despite being faulty, show that men and women can find the strength to carry on.

There's a lot in these pages that isn't funny and lots more that might be a little too real; so there's a danger that a story might actually cause offense.

In the event of offense: retreat to the nearest corner and wait for five minutes, chew the cud on it a bit more and if you can genuinely say after those three hundred seconds you are still actually offended then feel free come out swinging – I probably deserve it.

But you should know that offense really isn't my intention. At several times during my wobbly walk through life I've wondered if a good friend: a really good friend who you'd trust with your guitar or leave with a key to your house, did something awful – just how awful would it have to be so that I wouldn't stick by them? Or perhaps how gruelling could it be to me before I would have to step away?

I'm sure you would agree if you've suffered any hardship at all, even if it's the loss of your favourite stolen pint glass, that you find your ability to cope expands beyond that which you thought was acceptable.

So this is the take-away arrangement of this anthology. What you gain here can be spent elsewhere on some non-fictional pain that requires compassion - my thanks for going through the fictional pains to get here.

ASW, Cambridge 2012

Printed in Dunstable, United Kingdom

71469043R00067